Mixed D...

From that first game of mixed doubles on the badminton court, neither Michael and Theresa nor James and Lin are sure where they stand. Will Theresa fall for James's charm? Will Michael ever have the courage to ask her to be his girlfriend? Will Lin notice what James is up to? At Michael's 18th birthday party everything comes to a head . . .

Joel Smith

Mixed Doubles

LIONS · TRACKS

First published in Great Britain 1989 by
Lions Teen Tracks
8 Grafton Street, London W1X 3LA

Lions Teen Tracks is an imprint of
the Children's Division, part of
the Collins Publishing Group,

Printed and bound in Great Britain by
William Collins Sons & Co. Ltd, Glasgow

Chapter 1

"Michael, whatever you do, don't get up will you!"

June Dobson crashed her way through the living room door, struggling to bring in the family's ironing. She was also, as ever, struggling to bring up a couple of teenage children. Both tasks were inclined to cause her considerable frustration.

"What?" Michael was sprawled out on the sofa, doing what June always thought of as his impression of a basking seal.

"No really darling, it's alright. You just lie there . . . like you always do."

Gasping for a breath, June heaved a load of washing up onto the table. Michael, meanwhile, manipulated the TV remote control, his physical exercise for the evening, and pondered whether or not to change channels.

"It must be very tiring for you," said June, "all that growing you're doing."

Michael decided that he did want to see what was on BBC2, and was just about to press the button when the switch was snatched from his hand.

"No darling! Let me!" June rushed around the sofa. "I can do that for you . . . just like I do all the cooking, and the washing, and the ironing, and go to work all day to earn the money to keep you. Alright?"

"Sounds fair enough to me." Michael was quite used to these occasional outbursts.

"It's not a joke, Michael!" June tried unconvincingly to come over all stern and matriarchal. "I mean it's not just me. Your father was up and out of this house at five-thirty this morning, and he won't be in tonight until gone nine. Six and a half days a week he works! Even Lin works on Saturdays. You? You fell out of bed at quarter to nine, went to school, and staggered home, exhausted, at when, ten past eleven?"

"Twenty past!" Michael was indignant.

"Oh, sorry, been doing overtime have you?" June changed her tone. "Darling, won't you get into trouble with the school? I mean you're hardly ever there, are you?"

"I had one double lesson this morning." Michael explained it to her patiently, as if addressing a somewhat dim twelve year old, "and Sixth Form only have to turn up for lessons." This last claim was common enough practice at Warren Park, certainly in Michael's case, but was not strictly accurate.

"Well haven't you got any work to be getting on with?" June asked, hopefully.

"I've done it all," Michael replied, casually.

June was not convinced. "Michael, you're doing three A levels! You've got exams in the summer. How can you have 'done it all'?"

"I'm a genius aren't I?"

"Are you really Michael?" This was something June was less than convinced of. Michael was the only person who seemed to believe it.

"Definitely. The only one in this family. I must be. I'm the only one who doesn't spend all his time rushing around, knackering himself out."

"In that case," June looked down at him, "will you answer one question for me?"

"No problem." Michael stretched. June worried that this sudden exertion might do him lasting damage.

"Well," said June, "if you're so clever, why have you

6

got your jumper on back to front, eh?" She pulled the label under his chin to prove it. Michael put it back inside, but she pulled it back out again.

He would have been happy to let her have this little victory, but by now June was out to get her own back properly. Ignoring his cries to stop, she pulled Michael's arm behind his back, demanding that he surrender. The doorbell rang, but the struggle continued. He tried to push her off, but she prevented this by tickling him, knowing he had never had any resistance to that. Neither of them heard the bell ring again. Wearily, Michael submitted just as the bell rang a third time. His assailant stood up and went to peer through the gap in the curtains.

"It's James." She returned to her ironing. "Let him in, would you?"

"Why?" demanded the wounded Michael.

"Well he's your friend. He's come round to see you, hasn't he?"

"No," Michael replied. "Poor boy's finally gone terminally insane."

"Why?" June asked, as Michael got up and went to answer the door.

"He wants to give all his money away, so he's going out boozing with Cowface and that gang of hers." Michael disappeared through the front room door into the hall.

June called out after him: "Michael! don't talk about your sister like that!"

James was just about to ring again when Michael opened the door.

"Evening Mike."

Michael was Micky to everyone but his mother and father, except James, who for some strange reason insisted on calling him Mike. James, most often known as Jimmy, had lost count of the names Michael had for him: Jim, Jimbo, Jimmy Mack, McGarvey, Jock, and for special occasions, Great Daft Northern Scotch Catholic Pratt, or some variation on this theme.

Michael sniggered at the sight in front of him. James was more than used to all his taunts and sneers, and certainly did not care what Michael thought of the way he dressed: "You're just jealous, that's all," he taunted back, stepping past Michael into the hall.

"What? Of a refugee from a lager commercial like you!"

"Better than being an escapee from a jumble sale," James replied.

"Ah! I'm wounded, I'm wounded." Michael closed the front door.

"Where's Lin?"

"In the bathroom, probably. That's where she lives."

"Some of us like to look our best when we go out."

Michael considered the sister creature: "She sits in hot water for hours, and covers herself with herbs and spices. It's a wonder she doesn't come out casseroled." He dug James in the ribs. "Not that I thought you'd be interested in a tough old stew like her, eh? You normally go for something prettier, stupider, if that's possible, and younger, usually. I'm surprised you're not hanging around the swings down the park. That's where you find most of your girlfriends, isn't it?"

James's reputation as the School Romeo had become somewhat tarnished by rumours of his alleged preference for the younger age-range, rumours spread mainly by Michael.

"Mum doesn't know, though," Michael said. "I think she thinks you still want to molest her daughter."

"Why would she think that?"

"Because that's what I tell her."

"Mike."

"Jimbo?"

"Shut up."

Michael led James into the front room.

"Hello James darling." Everyone was "darling" to June. "You're looking very smart." Michael coughed loudly at this. "Yes he does, Michael," continued June, "which is more than you ever do."

"Thank you," James turned aside to Michael: "See, the Mums are always impressed, never mind what you think."

"Do I understand correctly, young man? That you've come to collect my lovely girl?"

"Lovely girl!" Michael exclaimed. "You've come to the wrong place, mate."

June put down the iron. She reached forward and covered Michael's head with a just-ironed pair of his own underpants. "Ignore him, I do." She continued with her chores. "No, I'm pleased," she said, "you're a great improvement on her usual taste."

"Don't know you very well, do she?" came the muffled comment from Michael.

Lin appeared in the doorway, decked out in her latest outfit, something loud and trendy which only a sixteen year old girl could ever have got away with. "Hi Jimmy."

"Evening Sexy," James said.

"Oh, do you like it?" She did an elegant twirl to show herself off.

Michael thought Lin was a bit like a three year old; a few sweet words and she'd show off to anyone. She and James were obviously made for each other.

9

June interrupted James and Lin's gooey eyed exchanges: "He'd better like it, the cost of it all."

James smiled. "For Lin to wear it, it's got to be good."

"Oh, Jimmy!" Lin grinned at her admirer.

Michael looked around for a bucket to be sick in. "Oh, Jimmy!" He hugged a cushion exaggeratedly: "I love it when you crawl."

"You know, Jackie and Sarah . . ." Lin meant James's sisters, "they're really lucky to have you for a brother. Me? I have to make do with Micky!"

"Just get stuffed, Cowface, OK?" Michael riposted with typical eloquence.

Lin turned to face her brother for the first time, but her anger quickly turned to amusement: "Mum, why has Micky got his knickers on his head?"

"Because that's the part of him that's full of you know what," suggested James.

"Hey, young man, don't you speak about my first born like that."

James was embarrassed. "Oh, sorry, I didn't mean . . ."

"No," said June, "it's just that that's my job. He's right, Michael, you're full of it."

Michael's face appeared from below the waistband of his underwear. "I think I'm doing rather well, considering what I have to put up with."

"Oh, good heavens," said June, "what do you have to put up with, you poor thing you?"

"Additives in food, lead in petrol, the crisis in education, you lot . . ." Michael listed.

June was not impressed: "You would have loved growing up when I was your age – coal-holes, outside lavatories, leftovers for tea, having to go out to work when you were fifteen! What a shock to your system all that would have been."

10

"Well, Mike, I'd really like to stay here and be miserable with you all evening, but we're meeting the others at eight," said Lin.

"Others?" June enquired.

"Just the Brownie Girls," said Lin, "Polly, Clare and Jill."

"Who?"

"Oh, you know Clare and Jill," Lin was getting tired of explaining this to her mum, "and Polly who was going out with Jimmy . . ."

"I thought that was Paula?" June was already getting confused, she wasn't even sure who Clare and Jill were.

"Yes! Paula is Polly." To Lin it was obvious that Paula O'Leary's name had been shortened to Polly, so as not to confuse her with any of the other Paulas; why on earth could Mum never understand?

"Paula is Polly?" repeated June, doubtfully.

"Yes," said Lin, "and Zed's coming too; Zahira, that is."

Zahira Qasim, pronounced Zeera, otherwise known as Z-Cars or Qasimodo, thought Michael. Nice girl. What was she doing boozing with the Brownies?

"Oh," said June, "I see. And who are you?"

"I'm Lin, aren't I!"

"Not Carmen, or Francesca, or Aphrodite or anything?"

"No, don't be stupid." In fact, officially, Lin was Belinda, but everybody had forgotten that.

"Is that all?" said James. "I thought you said . . ."

"Oh yes . . ." Lin remembered, "and Treez might be coming."

"Trees?" June was by now utterly bewildered.

Michael joined in: "Birch, willow, or horse chestnut?"

"Theresa Green . . ." Lin saw a chance to get back at her brother. "You know, Micky. The girl you fancy."

Michael went quiet. The way Lin had planned things, her

11

brother was supposed to be coming along as well. She had noticed that he was very interested in her friend Theresa, but knew he would never dare to go up to her and start a conversation in school. So, she had thought, bring them both along to the Argie Pub tonight. James could come to keep Michael company, and she could look after Theresa. That had been the plan. But Michael wouldn't come, and James on his own was a completely different proposition.

"Shall we go then?" James asked.

"OK," said Lin. "Bye Mum, bye Micky."

"Big Brother not invited?" June asked Michael.

"Big Brother doesn't want to come," he assured her.

"Well, have a nice time, both of you."

"Thanks," said James.

June continued: "Lin, don't drink too much, darling."

"I don't drink a lot," said Lin.

This was easily the funniest thing Michael had heard all evening, and he immediately collapsed into hysterics.

June let that one pass, but persisted: "And not too late either, or else your father will stay awake when he has to be up early. I want you in bed by midnight," she said.

"So does he, Mum," Michael suggested, looking at James.

June was not impressed. "I'm thinking of having him part-exchanged for an electric toothbrush. What do you think?"

"I'd say you'd be getting a bargain," said James. "G'night. See you tomorrow, Mike."

June said goodbye to James and Lin. "Bye bye children," said Michael, as they made their exit.

June watched them through the gap in the curtains as they strolled off down the path. "Wish I was going with them," she said, quietly to herself.

"Come on Treez, pub'll be shut by the time you get there."

Paula stood with Zahira at the kerbside, shouting for Theresa to catch up.

"Look, Polly, I'm not sure that I should be doing this."

"Why? Are you feeling ill?" Zahira took Theresa's arm as she crossed the road.

"No," said Theresa.

"Well, we'll soon put a stop to that, won't we?" said Paula. "Come on."

Paula O'Leary had been expelled from her previous school, Our Lady The Virgin, an internment camp for teenage girls run by secret police in drag. She had come into the Sixth Form at Warren Park, a large comprehensive with a very mixed intake, where it was well known that there were only two reasons girls were ever expelled from Our Lady The Virgin; for not being ladies, or the other possibility. In Paula's case, it was the first possibility that had got her kicked out, although school rumour was often inclined to say otherwise. She had gone to school one morning with a bottle of whisky and told the mother superior what she thought of her. That was all. She had had no difficulty gaining almost immediate admission to the Brownie Pack though, since they, unlike the nuns, greatly appreciated that sort of thing.

"Doesn't your dad mind you drinking, Zed?" Theresa asked.

"Mind! He'll probably cut me in half if he finds out."

"I might tell him," Paula threatened.

"He'd kill you too." Zahira liked Paula. As the only black girl in the 6th form, she was used to being given a hard time but she didn't mind teasing from Polly, who was equally awful to everybody. It made a nice change, Zahira thought.

13

"Then again, perhaps I won't," Paula added.

"Dad lets Rash go out wherever he wants," Zahira told them, referring to Rashid, her brother. "It's just me that's got to be a good little girl. He probably reckons he's going to marry me off to some kid from Karachi or Birmingham or somewhere." She spoke distastefully. Karachi and Birmingham were equally strange and distant places to Zahira.

"Oh, he couldn't make you do that if you didn't want to," Theresa said to her.

"Too right he couldn't! And he's not going to make me walk around in pyjamas, with a paper bag over me head, neither."

Zahira Qasim did lots of things that annoyed her parents. The main one at the moment was her insistence on conversing only in her own unique native tongue, a sort of Punjabi-Cockney that was all her own. In her mind, she wore her hair short and high to match her skirts and danced the night away with the pin-up boys in her teenage magazines. In reality, she had to stay in on Saturday nights to do her homework. She had only recently been allowed out at night during the week, and she planned to make up for lost time.

"But you're still a Moslem," said Theresa. "You're not allowed alcohol, are you?"

"So?" Zahira demanded. "Catholics aren't allowed pre-marital sex, but it don't stop you, does it Polly?"

"Look, I never said I'd done it," Paula was still trying to live down the consequences of the reputation that had preceded her to Warren Park, "I only said I might . . ."

"That's not what we've heard," whispered Zahira to Theresa.

"And when I said I might . . ." Paula continued.

"Jimmy said, what are we waiting for?" Zahira suggested.

14

The whirlwind romance and parting of Paula and James had already passed into school legend. Only James and the Brownie Pack knew what had really happened.

"If Jimmy's said anything like that, bragging to his mates, I'll get him for it."

"We don't know that he said anything." Theresa was trying to keep things calm.

"The sooner we can get you two both full members of the Brownies, the better," said Paula, "then I'll be able to put you straight."

The Brownie Pack was a secret society formed some years earlier by a number of wild, untamed Third Year girls. At the height of its power, it had ruled the playground and terrorised the toilets, where it had held its secret meetings. But now, with only four remaining members, it was a shadow of what it once had been. Zahira and Theresa were going to be evaluated tonight as potential new recruits. While Theresa was apprehensive about the prospect, Zahira was already looking forward to it.

"You don't deny it, though?" Zahira needled Paula skilfully.

"Look!" Paula's patience was coming under considerable strain. "Whatever me and him had is had, OK? What do they call it in French?"

"Finis?" suggested Zahira.

"No," said Paula.

"Passé?" suggested Theresa.

"No! Wotsit; that homework I couldn't do?"

Polly couldn't do any of the homework, thought Theresa.

"Past tense," Paula declared, triumphantly. "That's it. All references to him and me in the past tense, please."

"Polly's love life in the past tense from now on," Theresa noted, dutifully.

"And when I said I might . . ." Paula was now able to return to what she had wanted to say, "I only meant might."

"Polly's love life in the conditional tense," Zahira proposed.

"Zahira's head down the bog, if she's not careful!"

Reaching Clare Hunter's house, their initial destination, the three girls approached the front porch. Paula rang the bell. "Clare, on the other hand," she said, "not only would; she has! But I'm not even supposed to be telling you that. Oh. Hi, Clare!"

Clare's head appeared round the edge of the door: "Hi Polly babes. Where's Lin?"

"She said she'd come on her own." Lin had not told the other girls about her match-making plans.

Clare "Babes" Hunter would certainly have had little difficulty getting herself expelled from Our Lady, had she gone there. She was the sort of girl who could cause mayhem in a school corridor, as people of both sexes stopped and stared and bumped into each other and brick walls as she walked past. She specialised in making quivering wrecks out of young male teachers. They none of them dared give her a detention, that was for sure.

Jill Bryce's head appeared above Clare's, which was quite appropriate, Paula thought, since they were so inseparable that she often thought of them as a four-legged, two-headed monster. "Hi Polly, Zed, and Treez!" said Jill, "I've got that English essay to give you back."

"Oh, good," said Theresa, "did you get the main points of the argument?"

"Didn't understand a word of it. Just copied it but in a different order. You can explain it to me down the pub."

Young Lady was not a term many people would use

to describe "JB" Bryce either, unless they were being sarcastic. She was warm, kind, generous and considerate, to those who knew her. The only things wrong with her, in fact, were that she had a mouth like a sewage outfall pipe and the obedience in class of an escaped mink. She had calmed down a bit in her old age of late, but she was still hated by all teachers as the sometime outlaw queen of Middle School. She was only staying on to get herself into college to study mechanics.

The girls set off down Clare's path together. They wondered if they ought to wait for Lin their leading light before starting on the drink, but then decided not to bother, since she wouldn't have waited for them.

Phil Dobson smiled as he opened the doors of his bus to two familiar passengers. "Hello, James. Everything alright?"

"No." James climbed aboard. "She's had us miss three buses; says she only travels on yours."

"Hi Dad." Lin spoke from the pavement.

James put his money in the box. "I think I know why that is," Phil said, giving James a ticket.

"Hi Dad," Lin climbed aboard. Phil closed the bus doors and pulled away from the stop. Lin stood by the ticket dispenser as he drove off down the street, waiting, she hoped, for a free ride. James stood aside.

"Don't you hi Dad me. Where are you going?"

"Top of the High Street."

"OK, 35 pence."

"I go free."

"Do you? How come?"

"Because you let me."

"Sweetheart, I've explained to you before. I do not

17

own this bus. It is not a taxi. I do not collect the fares for myself."

"I go free," repeated Lin.

"The bus company lets you travel free, they give you a pass," said Phil. "Where is it?"

"I told you! I lost it."

"So it's 35 pence then, isn't it?"

"No it's not."

"Are you refusing to pay, young lady?"

"Yes! What you going to do about it?"

"Well in that case, Miss, I shall have to take your name and address."

"But you know me!"

"Your mother will get a letter from the office for non-payment of fare."

"Well, that would be your fault, wouldn't it?"

"My name won't be on the letter."

"I've got a witness."

"James will back me up."

"No he won't. He's my friend."

"He's a regular guest in my house," said Phil. "He knows what's good for him."

"Jimmy!"

"Here . . ." James reached into his pocket, "I'll pay for her."

"You won't get it back, I'll tell you that."

James put some more money down.

"There you go," said Phil.

"Thanks." James took the ticket, licked it, and stuck it on Lin's forehead.

"Nice outfit, Sweetheart, where are you going in it?"

"Mind your own business."

It was so predictable, thought Phil. First it was Hi Dad, lovely to see you Dad, give me what I want Dad.

Now it was get lost, hate you, mind your own business, Dad.

"Only down the Argie Pub." James was still trying to be helpful. Never get on the wrong side of their parents, he thought.

"So you'll be home about half past eleven then?" Phil suggested.

"Don't know," said Lin. "I might walk the streets for a while. Pick up a few men. Buy some drugs or something."

"I'll bring her home," James promised.

"Thank you son," said Phil. "No Michael then?"

"Par for the course," said James.

"Oh, at home laying down for a change, is he?"

"You guessed."

"Can't you find him a girl or something, James?"

"Who'd want him?"

In spite of everything, Lin still had a soft spot for her brother, and it wasn't seven foot of quicksand. "I could fix him up if he wanted, Dad, but he's just not interested."

"Leave him alone," said James. "He'll get off his backside when he's ready."

"I expect so," Phil said, "but I just have these visions of him laying there, uninterested, until he's about 32 or something. I mean who does he think he is? Prince Charles?"

James and Lin spent the whole ride talking up front with Lin's father. Soon, they reached the top of the High Street.

"Here you are." Phil opened the doors. "Have a good evening, won't you."

"Thanks Dad, bye."

Her father gave her a wink: "Bye Sweetheart. See you around some time, James."

"Bye," said James. "Watch out for fare-dodgers."

"Righto."

"And don't work too hard," James added.

"Son, I just wish I didn't have to."

Phil closed the bus doors and drove off.

"We're early." Lin stared across the street to the Argie Pub.

"Listen, would you rather go somewhere else?" James took hold of her gently by the elbows.

"Like where?"

"I don't know. How about down by the river? I know a good bench," he suggested, "or there's under the bridge?"

Lin had been going out with boys ever since she had found out what they were. She had led a sheltered life, her brother used to say; bus shelters, bicycle shelters, park bench shelters . . . but she wasn't as bad as some. She might try to scrounge a lift to where she was going, but she always had the bus fare to get herself back alone, if necessary. It was like Dirty Harry's Magnum; it was there in her pocket, and she wasn't afraid to use it. All Brownie Girls knew that one.

"Jimmy, we've been through it all before." Lin sounded just like her father, telling her off. "I'm not going into any dark corners with you. I know what you're like."

"Not yet you don't . . ." James unsuccessfully tried to demonstrate what he was like.

"Stop it!"

"I haven't even started, yet." He took hold of her gently this time. "Like to, though."

There were strict rules to the games James liked to play, and the important thing was not to win but to take part. It was the thrill of the chase as much as anything he was after, and when it came to chasing girls, he knew the score; you chased them until they caught you.

"I don't want to be just another name on your list," Lin told him, "I'll still be your friend. But if you want me to be more than that . . ."

"Tie a knot in it, I know."

"Change your ways," she corrected him. "You're not going to love me and leave me, Jimmy, like you do with all the others."

"I might not ever change, then you'd be out of luck."

She stroked his forearms and made him let go of her. "Come on, it's cold out here," she said, and they both headed towards the open door.

The Copacobana was a sort of wine and cocktail bar, where they weren't terribly strict about not serving young-ish-looking drinkers; a regular haunt for the Brownie Girls for some time now. The bar had used to be called Tangoes. When it had opened, its walls had been covered with pictures of Ardiles, Villa and Evita. Then came the Hostilities and, after a couple of nasty incidents, the bar shut. When it eventually reopened, the name had been changed, and the pictures were of Brazilian footballers and racing drivers. But everyone still called it the Argie Pub, even those, like Lin, who were too young to know why.

James and Lin got their drinks, then went to sit down in sight of the entrance, so that the others could spot them. As Lin sat sipping her pina colada, James was already beginning to feel queasy with fear at the impending severe loss of hard-earned tenners.

"I'm not buying you another one of them," he told her.

Oh yes you are, she thought, sucking her straw, already

thinking of ways she was going to make this happen.

"What was that you were saying about Mike?" James was feeling a little exposed out on the floor, instead of in his favoured position in one of the booths, where you could get up to all sorts of things, he recalled. No chance tonight, he thought.

"What about him?"

"That he fancies the Megaswot?"

"You mean you haven't noticed?" Lin found that hard to believe. She thought it was so obvious she found it difficult not to laugh.

"I've not seen," said James.

"Oh come on, he can't take his eyes off her."

"I haven't seen. I think I'd notice if he did."

"No, well, he stops when he thinks you've spotted him," said Lin. "He's like that, my brother. Oh, here they are. Now they might not want you here, so just be quiet and drink your drink . . . and leave this to me."

The five girls came to the table, all eyes on James.

"Hey," said Paula. "I thought this was just girls. No boyfriends."

"Jimmy's not a boyfriend!" Lin ridiculed the suggestion. "And he's buying everybody pina coladas!"

"He stays," said Jill.

"Yeah!" Zahira agreed.

Lin smiled at James. Under the table, James kicked her on the shin, and reached for his wallet.

Back at home, Michael was still monopolising the sofa.

"I'm going to have a bath darling," said June, coming in from putting the ironing board away.

"Alright." Michael was not quite sure why she was telling him this.

"Are you alright?" she asked.

"Yeah."

"How's your throat?"

"OK today."

"And what about your illness?"

"Eh?"

"The infliction that forces you to spend your whole life in a horizontal position."

"Oh, leave it Mum."

"OK." said June. "Just move your leg occasionally, or the cat might think you're dead and try to eat you."

It did not take the girls long to polish off six pina coladas. Only Theresa had any trouble, and Zahira was happy to help finish hers.

"Right, what are we having? Red or white?" Jill got down to business.

"What's the difference?" asked Zahira.

Paula though it was almost touching. "Did you hear that? Dear, sweet child."

"There is no difference at all," said Clare, "provided you drink enough of the stuff."

"You'd know all about that, my darlin'," Jill replied.

"At least I can hold my drink," Clare responded. "I'm not the one who gives free strip shows when she's pissed, Babe."

"No," said Jill. "You'd never do anything for free, would you?"

"There is a difference." Theresa interrupted the two girls' friendly exchange: "Red gives you more of a hang-over."

23

"You what?" said Jill.

"How many hangovers have you had then, Treez?" Clare liked to think she was quite an expert on the subject of hangovers.

"Red is heavier," Theresa explained. "It contains more impurities, and it's the impurities that give you the hangover, not the alcohol."

"Daddy's a doctor," Lin explained.

Theresa corrected her: "Mum's a doctor, Dad's a medical researcher."

"Don't suppose they had much difficulty making you then." Jill was a bit cold, reacting to Theresa's too immaculate diction.

"We'll have some of each then, shall we?" said Lin, practical as ever.

Lin brought the wine, and the gossip, too, soon flowed. The conversation was led by Lin, who always worked on the principal of let's-talk-about-who's-not-here. They talked about boys and eyeliners, and other things Theresa found totally uninteresting. Zahira almost screamed with laughter at times, as Clare and Jill recounted details of who was doing what with whom. Paula seethed quietly much of the time to herself. She didn't want James at what she had been led to believe was going to be a strictly girls' gathering. James tried to steer the conversation onto his favourite subject, himself. Lin tried to involve Theresa in the conversation, but she dismissed everything out of hand. Clare and Jill began to get irritated by the stuck-up rich girl from the snooty part of town. After half an hour of this, Lin decided that it was time for her to act. She gulped down what was left of her drink. "I've got to go to the loo," she said. "You coming, Treez?"

"No, I'm alright."

"Oh c'mon." Lin was quite insistent. "I want you to try some of this new mascara."

"Lin! You know I don't wear make-up."

Lin was beginning to get agitated. "Well you can wipe it off afterwards, can't you? Come on!"

Theresa was grabbed by the arm, and led to the Ladies.

"There are three great unanswered questions known to man," James announced. "Is there a God? Is there life after death? And why do girls never go to the lavatory on their own?"

"Honestly, Treez, can't you take a hint?"

"Lin, I was always told not to get into cars with strange men, and girls who want me to come to the toilet with them seem just as suspicious to me."

"It's because I want to talk to you."

"Well, we can talk anytime," Theresa said.

"No, I have to see you now."

"What about?"

"When do you have to be in tonight?"

"I don't."

"You don't! You mean you can stay out all night?"

"Well, now, I have to let the dog out, or else she'll make a mess. There's no one home; Mum's on nights, Dad's at a conference, and Gordon's back at University now."

"Do they often leave you with the house to yourself?"

"Sometimes. Why?"

"Well we could have a party round your place."

"Oh no, I don't know about that."

"Shut up. You don't come to any of our parties, so we'll have one round yours; that way you'll have to come along."

Theresa looked worried. "Oh, I'm only joking," said Lin. "If you could ask and see if it's alright, that would be great, but if not, don't worry. Anyway, not what I wanted to talk about. I wanted to make a suggestion."

"I don't like make-up Lin, it makes me feel uncomfortable."

"Not about make-up, stupid. Listen, you know my brother?"

"Micky?"

"Only brother I've got, yes. Do you like him?"

"Well, he's alright." Suddenly, the penny dropped. "What do you mean by 'like'?" The alarm bells were starting to ring in Theresa's head. There were three things in life she wanted to avoid at the moment: distractions from her work, infectious diseases and boys. She thought there was probably a close connection between all three.

"He's not bad looking, is he?" Lin suggested.

"Forget it Lin." Theresa made for the door, but Lin held her back.

"Oh, Treez, I know you'll like Micky. Come back for coffee tonight and meet him."

"But I see your brother every day," Theresa said. "We do go to the same school. Well, I go there; he sometimes visits, doesn't he?"

"I know, but I want you to meet him socially, get to know him . . ."

"Get fixed up with him?"

"If you like."

"No thanks Lin." Theresa turned to exit once again.

Theresa and Lin had once been inseparable best friends, but times had changed and they had drifted apart. Now they were in the Sixth Form together, they were becoming close again, despite Theresa being an 'A' Level student and

Lin a one-year retake candidate. There was also Theresa's non-membership of the Brownie Pack, something Lin hoped to rectify, if only her friend would do something wicked enough to gain entry. Things could have been so different; they had both been promising athletes in earlier years. Theresa had given it up, preferring to concentrate on her books. Lin, meanwhile, had missed an important district selection meeting because the previous night she had been to a party where she had broken her personal best for Cinzano and lemonade, an event not yet on the Olympic programme.

Theresa stepped out into the bar, and was on her way back to her seat, when her arm was grabbed from behind. She was pulled back into the toilet.

"Oh, Lin!" Theresa protested meekly.

"Shut up. Sit down!" Lin opened a cubicle. Theresa sat down. Lin stepped into the cubicle with her, and bolted the door.

"What if someone comes in?" Theresa was shouting in a whisper.

"You worry about everything," said Lin, "that's your trouble. What happened to you? You used to be great fun, before you turned into a Megaswot!"

"We're different, Lin," said Theresa. "I discovered Thomas Hardy, and you discovered pina coladas."

"Who's he?"

"Who?"

"Thomas Thingy?" Lin hadn't heard of anybody at school by that name.

Theresa quoted *Tess of the D'Urbervilles*: "Why so often the coarse appropriates the finer thus? Morality good enough for divinity is scorned by human nature, and it therefore does not mend the matter."

Lin thought that sounded beautiful, whatever it meant.

"Oh Treez, the way you talk, you have definitely got to meet Micky."

"What for?"

"Because he's a boy, for crying out loud!"

"Boys, Lin, are only mouth, trousers, and wandering hands."

"Yeah, I know," said Lin, ruefully, "but they aren't half lovely, though."

Theresa opened the cubicle. She was not going to carry on with this any more.

"They are made from frogs and snails and puppy dogs' tails," she said, "and they have balls instead of brains."

"How do you know?" Lin demanded. "You been out with any boys?"

Theresa avoided answering. "I am not the complete innocent you seem to think I am, Lin," she said.

"No, you've been carrying on with Thomas Thingy, haven't you?"

Theresa couldn't resist it. "Yes! I was up till gone midnight in bed with him last night!"

Theresa left Lin not quite sure what to make of that. She got back to her seat, and swigged half a glass of wine in one mouthful. Frogs and snails and puppy dogs' tails, she thought to herself. "Oh hello Jimmy," she said, noticing him looking at her, "I was just thinking about you." James did not know what on earth she meant. She held up her empty glass. "Any more of this?"

Phil Dobson hung his jacket up in the hall and wandered into the front room, already half-asleep. "Hello son," he said to Michael. "Where's your mother?"

"She went for a bath nearly an hour ago. Hasn't been seen since."

Phil stood in the doorway and hollered: "You in the bath, June?"

"I've just got out," came the cry back.

Phil called back: "Alright. I'll be up in a minute!"

Michael was watching the news. Phil tried to think of something to say to him: "Football on tonight?"

"Tomorrow. Third round replay."

"Oh. Arsenal should win that, I reckon."

"Yeah."

"Your sister's on the town again?"

"Mmmm."

Phil's patience ran out: "It would be nice if you could try a bit more to communicate!" he shouted.

Michael said nothing.

"Fourteen hours I've been at work today," Phil shouted, "fourteen bloody hours!"

"What's the matter?" June came in, still rubbing her hair with a towel.

"All he does is eat and sleep! Can't even pass the time of day! I get more out of his mate than I do out of him."

"Michael! Sit up!" June rarely raised her voice, but when she did Michael always responded. He sat up. "If you do nothing else in this house," she said, "can you at least remember your manners?"

"I'm going to bed." Phil felt full of frustration whenever he tried to get some sense out of Michael. Michael would not have been half so scared of his father, if he'd known just how scared Phil was of him, and the razor tongue that could put Phil down like a fly swat.

"I'll be up," said June, as Phil turned and stamped out of the room. Michael turned back to the television. She switched it off and pulled the plug out. "He blows his top because he cares about you."

"I know." When Phil blew his top, Michael couldn't help feeling four years old. They could only communicate with each other these days via June.

June sat down in the chair opposite Michael. "Not long till you're eighteen," she said, "a young adult."

"No more presents?"

"Not so many. Getting older becomes less to celebrate after a while."

"I want an RPG-7," said Michael.

"I'll have to ask your father about that. He knows about motorbikes."

"It's a hand-held rocket launcher," Michael explained. "They use them in Beirut."

"If I see one cheap in Sainsbury's, I'll think about it." June could see why Michael made Phil so angry at times. "If you were at work, I'd charge you rent." She was determined to at least try to have a serious conversation. "Lin too. You'd be making a contribution, so you'd have a say in how this house is run. I think that would be fair, don't you?"

"Suppose so."

June persisted: "If you were still a child, though, I'd want you to do as you were told. But as things stand Michael . . . well I don't know where we stand. Have I the right to tell you what to do or not? Have I?"

Michael didn't answer her question. "Say sorry to Dad for me?" he said instead.

"I will," said June; "but will you make more of an effort in future?"

"Yeah," Michael half-whispered.

"Everything OK at school?"

"Fine," he said. Not true.

Did he want to go out with Treez? Lin had asked him the other day. He had said no, vigorously. He didn't want to be the latest running joke for the hideous ferret pack, as he called Lin's gang. Plus he was afraid of what Treez might say, afraid she'd tell him to get lost. He was always afraid of them saying that; which was why he'd never managed to ask one out so far. He stuck to watching them across crowded rooms, dreaming.

"Not crying over any girls, then?" June asked.

"No," he said. She certainly wasn't going to get that out of him.

"Why not? You ought to be at your age, you know?" She smiled at him. "Goodnight darling." She kissed him, and left him on his own.

"You're not like the rest of these girls, are you, Treez?"

"Aren't I?"

"I bet you passed more exams than any of them, eh?"

"Yes. I expect so."

"I'll tell you something, Treez: I normally can't stand 'A' Level Girls. Girlie Swots, I call them. I suppose it's because I find them a bit threatening. You know, a bit too clever for me?"

"Yes, probably."

"But I go for brains as well as beauty, and you've obviously got both."

No response.

"How about you? What do you go for in a boy?" James was hoping for some clues.

"I don't 'go' for boys," Theresa answered him contemptuously without bothering to look at him.

James was getting nowhere, and he knew it. He had tried all his best lines, but all Theresa did was sit, look and drink. He watched anxiously as she finished another glass of wine. "She's been knocking it back like nobody's business," he said to Lin. "Will she be alright?"

"I don't know," said Lin. "I don't think she's used to it."

Lin had noticed that James had been talking to Theresa for quite a while, without getting much response. At last he had met his match, she thought – Old Smoothie Tongue himself versus the winner of this year's Miss Concrete Knickers of the Sixth Form title by a unanimous vote. James usually won by a knockout, but Theresa was a mile ahead on points. She knew exactly what he was after, and felt totally uninterested. She was just going to sit there and enjoy watching him trying it on.

"Speaking of drunks . . ." Paula looked across the bar.

Clare and Jill quickly got up to retrieve Zahira, who was looking for the toilet, but had only managed to find a door-less alcove. "I'm alright, really I am," she said to a large rubber-plant.

"Zed my dear, you are as alright as a newt," said Jill. "Come on."

"This way Zed, Babes," said Clare. One at each elbow, they guided her back on course.

Just then, Zahira noticed that the whole pub was revolving: "I'm sorry," she said. "I'm sorry."

"Oh stop it. You get your first Brownie badge for tonight," said Clare.

"Brownie badge!" Zahira giggled, spotting Clare's unintentional racial reference.

"What? Oh yes, very good," said Jill.

"What will the second badge be for?" Zahira asked, as they approached the Ladies.

"For getting off with a decent bloke, but I'd leave that one for now if I were you." Clare kicked the door open. They disappeared behind it.

"You OK Treez?" Lin didn't think that she was. She

was already resigned to having one candidate for the black coffee treatment before bedtime.

Theresa nodded, staring into empty space. She sipped some more wine. She liked the taste. It made everything around her seem soft and warm.

"Are you sure?" Lin put a hand on her shoulder.

Theresa said nothing. She thought of all the girls who would go weak at the knees if Jimmy McGarvey said so much as hello to them. The School Romeo had been chatting her up, and she could take it, or leave it. Of course she was OK. She turned to James, smiled, and quickly resumed staring into space. She wasn't going to give him any clues, she thought, not realising that he thought she just had. Keep trying, I'm playing hard to get, he thought she was telling him.

"She'll be alright." James talked across Theresa to Lin, as if there were no one between them.

Lin had made a decision. "Polly, look after Treez." She stood up and took James's hand: "Come on," she said, and led him to the door.

Theresa spoke only softly, but it made them both stop dead in their tracks. "Wait," she said. James and Lin both turned around. "It's late," she said. "Will someone take me home, please?"

Lin bundled James out of the pub before he could say anything.

"This is more like it," said James, "I've never been dragged out into a dark alley and ravished before. No, tell a lie, there was that time at Big Dave's party . . ."

Lin ignored him. "Tell me," she said, "what do you think of Treez?"

"Why should I tell you?"

33

"Because she's my friend, and because I'm asking."

"She's nice. Not what she seems."

"What does she seem then?"

"A great stuck-up Girlie Swot who wanders round school with her head in a book all the time. But underneath it all, she's a very attractive character," he said. "And she's got a right pair of nice ones on her. I'd like to see more of her."

"What? more of her character, or her figure?"

"Both. Why? Are you telling me to lay off?"

"Asking."

"Request noted," said James.

"She needs to be brought out of her shell." Lin was trying to sound constructive.

"I agree," said James. "Good job I'm around, n'it?"

"You know what I said about Micky?"

"Yeah. So what?"

"Well I've had a word with her," Lin claimed, "and she likes Micky too."

"I like him," James told her. "He's a good mate."

"Micky's never had a proper girlfriend."

"Don't I know it."

"You could probably have half the girls in the school if you wanted." Lin was trying to drop hints.

"I probably have had," James replied casually. "Only one girl I can think of who I can't have, and she told me I should find someone else."

"Theresa really likes Micky."

"Then what have you got to worry about?" James said. "Come on. It's cold out here, remember?"

"What, in the name of hell did you say that for?" Paula asked.

34

"It's late. It's dark." Theresa sounded meek.

"You do realise that was a come-on?"

Theresa resumed staring, but her mood had changed. She hadn't meant to say it like that. Replaying it in her mind, she realised it really did sound like "why don't you come back to my place?"

She put her nearly full glass of wine down on the table. She'd already had one too many.

"I bet you've never even been with a boy, have you?" Paula suggested.

"No." Theresa was still staring, keeping calm, but beginning to realise that she had dropped herself right in it. What should she do? Say sorry? Tell him to get lost? She didn't dare ask.

"Well if Jimmy's what you're after," said Paula; "you could do a lot worse. But don't give him the wrong idea."

Theresa pushed her glass as far away as it would go. She didn't want to give anyone the wrong idea, she thought.

"He's not so bad, really," Paula told her, "so long as you know where you are with him." Theresa wasn't asking, but Paula decided she was in need of at least a little advice: "They come in three sorts, boys," she said. "Those that take whatever liberties they can get away with, those that want to take liberties, but won't push their luck (rare those), and those like Jimmy who'll take liberties, but say sorry afterwards."

"You missed out one group," Theresa said.

"Did I?"

"Those who don't know the first thing to do."

"They don't count," said Paula. "Are you drunk?"

"Yes."

Theresa had been drunk before. On holiday. But this was different. After thinking that the situation was nothing

35

she couldn't handle, now she realised that she didn't even know where she was and she felt scared.

"I live near you," said Paula. "I'll take you home."

The door of the Ladies flew open, and out danced Zahira, pursued by Clare and Jill.

"Come back, Zed," cried Jill.

"No! I'm alright." Zahira collided with a table. "I'm free. No silly pyjama clothes. No paper bag over me head." Then she saw him: "Jimmy!"

James and Lin had reappeared through the doorway. Seeing James, Zahira made a beeline for him. "Lin . . ." She rebounded off another table, "how many Brownie points do you get for a big, long, snog?"

She fell into his arms. He gave her back to Clare and Jill, who took her away and sat her down.

"I'm having to fight them off tonight, Pol," he said to Paula, and gave a little wink to Theresa, sitting next to her.

"I'm taking her home, Jimmy," said Paula, firmly.

"Are you? Is that right Treez?" he asked.

"Yes it is!" said Lin. "Thanks Polly."

"Well who am I taking home then?" James demanded, preening himself.

"Me," said Lin. "You promised my Dad, remember?"

"Oh yeah."

"And after that . . ." said Lin.

"I could show you what you're missing." James grabbed her.

"You might have to take Zed home as well," she said, pushing him away, "after we've sobered her up."

"Shall I show her instead, then?"

"I don't know, you'll have to ask her dad when I phone him." Lin picked up her bag and coat, and got ready to leave. The others followed suit. Clare and Jill

36

attended to Zahira, as if dressing an overgrown baby. She had surely passed the test, and would be told the news tomorrow that she too was now a Brownie Girl. When she was ready, the two girls gave Zahira to James, who took her arm. Half-opening her bleary eyes, she looked up at him, and contentedly leaned her head against his shoulder. James propped her up, zipped up his jacket with his free hand, and considered how much lighter his wallet felt compared with the start of the evening. His tenners had flown away. He looked for Theresa, but she had disappeared briefly into the Ladies.

Theresa had not passed, the girls later decided. She had managed her share of the drink alright, but had not ended up like Zahira, talking to a shrub. Nor had she passed out, thrown up, or danced on the table as others had done in their time. She would have to try again, they decided.

"OK Gang," said Lin. "I'll see you all tomorrow in school."

"School?" said Jill, "what's that?"

"That big grey building at the bottom of the hill, remember?" said Clare.

"Oh yeah, that," said Jill, wearily.

"Goodnight everybody," said Paula, starting off a complete round of goodnights from all present who were still conscious.

The group left the pub, and set off in their different directions.

On the way home, Theresa tried to think who was the best looking boy at school, but couldn't decide what that meant.

"Hello, is that Mr. Qasim?" Lin said down the phone.

"This is Lin Dobson, Zahira's friend from school."

James brought a large pot of coffee in from the kitchen on a tray with three cups, and placed it on the table in front of Zahira.

"Yes, she's fine," said Lin, as James held a full cup of black coffee to Zahira's lips. She took the cup, and inhaled from its vapours. James tipped the cup and made her take a mouthful.

"No, there's nothing wrong. It's just that we missed the bus, and there won't be another till after midnight . . ."

In contrast to earlier in the evening, Zahira was now reluctant to drink. James pointed to Lin on the phone to her father and urgently gestured that she should keep swallowing.

"Film? Oh yes the film, that was good. All us girls enjoyed it . . . Oh yes, Mr. Qasim, we often go out together . . . Oh you know, to the pictures, ice skating, the squash club . . ."

James brought Lin a coffee.

"Yes, just us girls." She took the cup. James indicated that he could see her nose getting bigger as she told more lies. She pushed him away: "No," she said, "no bars."

James returned to Zahira. She had managed to drink half a cup. She looked at James mournfully, and offered him what remained. He shook his head, and refilled her cup to the brim.

"Well some are like that, Mr. Qasim, but you don't want to believe all the stories . . . Where? Ash Crescent, just off Warren Hill Lane. Yes, that's right, near the school." Zahira's father said he would be round immediately to collect her. Lin gestured to James to speed up the treatment: "Number 11, yes, see you then." She put the phone down. "In ten minutes!" she called to James.

"You hold her down, I'll get the funnel."

Michael appeared in the doorway, dressed in pyjama trousers and an old T-shirt. "Any coffee left?" he asked.

"I'll get another cup," said Lin, and went to the kitchen.

Michael leant over the back of the sofa: "Have a jolly time, did you?" he asked James.

"OK."

"This yours?" Michael nodded at Zahira, who had fallen asleep.

"No," said James. "I'm dead fussy; they've got to be awake."

"Got any money left?" Michael asked. James said nothing. Michael smiled.

Lin returned and poured Michael a coffee. She put some music on, volume down low, and sat with the other three. When Zahira's father arrived to take her home, he seemed to accept her tiredness at face value.

"Phew," thought Lin.

James drank his coffee and got up to leave. Lin showed him to the door, where he managed to grab a goodbye kiss. She watched him walk out of sight and went back in to talk to her brother.

"Listen," she said; "it's about Treez."

Chapter 2

Phil Dobson had set off early, as usual, leaving June some time on her own before Michael or Lin emerged from their rooms. She fed the cat, threw out the old newspapers, had a quick glance at the day's paper, and took her own and Phil's ironed clothes upstairs. In the kitchen some coffee cups had been left out, washed but left on the draining board. She rinsed them, wiped them and put them away. She had just put the kettle on to make some tea when Lin appeared in the doorway, yawning, wearing only a shirt and panties. "Tea," she said, between yawns. "Lovely."

"Good evening, was it?" June asked.

"Yeah. Great." June did not think she sounded very enthusiastic.

"Headache?" June asked, by which she meant "did you have too much to drink?"

"No. Fine," said Lin, unconvincingly. June gave Lin a cup of tea. She drank most of it in one go, without drawing breath.

"I had to be in at ten o'clock when I was sixteen," said June, "or else my mum wouldn't cook me any dinner . . ."

Lin opened the fridge, still on automatic pilot, and took out a yoghurt.

". . . I had to stay up in my room with a plate of bread and dripping," June continued.

"Quite right too. Nan says you were always a naughty girl."

"Yes, I was." June thought that Lin didn't know the half of it, "by the standards of the time. But they were different times."

"Well they had to be careful in those days, didn't they? What with Jack The Ripper roaming the streets."

June turned around so that she could give Lin a smack in the mouth, or something, but she had gone to answer the door. June guessed who it was at this early hour: "Lin!" she called, "I wish you'd put your dressing gown on in the mornings."

"Hi Sonny." When Lin opened the door, a small figure stood on the step below her.

"Is he up yet?" Roland asked, as he stepped inside.

"Of course he isn't," said Lin, shutting the door behind him. Roland headed straight for the kitchen.

"Hello Roland darling," said June.

Lin came following in behind Roland: "Oh, Mum! You're the only person in the world who calls him Roland!"

Roland was the same age as Michael, but was still in the Lower Sixth, his last chance to pass some exams. He looked younger than most Fourth Years, and often acted more like one of them. He had always been Michael's best friend, and had been adopted by Lin and the Brownie Girls as a sort of pet. They had done all sorts of things to him, between them, but for badge purposes they had decided that he did not count as a boy. He was quite harmless.

"You're the one that's embarrassing him, young lady."

June had hoped that Lin would stop running round the house half-undressed after puberty. Michael would throw furniture at Lin if she ever caught sight of him less than fully dressed and he went into a panic if June ever caught him with his shirt not tucked in. June wished she knew why they had turned out so different.

"Oh, Sonny doesn't mind," said Lin, wandering past him out into the hall.

"Seen it all before," said Roland, dismissively. That was quite possible, June thought.

June addressed Roland: "I was just going to throw Michael out of bed, but you can do that for me now."

"OK," said Roland. "Any food?"

June did not know whether or not Roland had any breakfast before he left home in the mornings but thought it most unlikely. It was possible, she sometimes thought, that he had nothing when he went home either. He was that small. She didn't like to ask, but she did worry about him: "Come on," she said. "We'll find something."

June opened the cupboard: "Let's see," she said, "there's cornflakes?"

Roland took the box: "Do you know that there's more nourishment in a cornflake box than in the cornflakes?"

"Well you can have the box if you like," said June, pouring a cup of tea for Michael.

Roland took a bite out of the top of the cornflake box, and chewed it thoughtfully: "Tastes a bit like cardboard," he said. "But it must be good. Look, it says here, 'this box contains iron, vitamins A, B1, B2, D, and calcium for healthy bones and teeth'." He took another bite. June poured a bowl of the contents and a cup of tea: "Here." She handed both to Roland. "Take this up to Michael, please. I'll do you both some toast when you get him down here."

"Got any Marmite?" Roland asked.

"I've got it all, hidden away somewhere at the back of the cupboard. If Michael's in one of his difficult moods, feel free to throw the tea over him, won't you?"

In the hall, Lin watched as Roland made his way up the stairs, contentedly slurping Michael's cornflakes, and munching on a piece of cardboard. Embarrass *him*, she thought? That was a good one.

Roland kicked open the door and entered Michael's earthquake-devastated bedroom. He half-opened the curtains: "Micky," he said.

No response.

Roland put the tea down at the side of Michael's bed, but continued to suck up cornflakes and milk as he wandered around the room. He scanned around in the semi-darkness and finally found what he was looking for, half-hidden under a pile of clothes. Very carefully, he placed the personal stereo headphones over Michael's ears. Digging through a pile of tapes, he found a particularly noisy one, and wound it to the beginning. He plugged Michael in, switched on, and retired at a safe distance.

Michael woke with a deep, angry moan. He wrenched off the headphones, and when he saw who had arranged the unwelcome alarm call, threw the little stereo across the room, smashing it and just missing Roland's head

"You getting up or what?" Roland asked, ducking.

Michael looked at his watch: "No. Get lost!" He retreated back under the sheet.

"Lazy pig."

Michael's muffled voice came from under the bed-clothes. "I'm not lazy. I am in tune with my biorhythms. My biorhythms say I should stay in bed today."

"Mine say that every day," Roland claimed.

"Yes, and you don't listen to them, do you? No wonder you don't grow any bigger. If you played truant a bit more, you could be six foot tall."

Michael reached out and switched on the radio. The traffic report said there were long tailbacks on the M25. "There are always long tailbacks on the M25," he said. "Endless queues of Ford Sierras, stretching to infinity. You could join them, if you passed your exams like a good little boy."

"Not much chance of that," said Roland.

Michael thought that soon everyone in Westone would have a Ford Sierra with a sunroof and metallic paint. They could park it outside the semi-detached house they would be paying for for the rest of their lives, drive it to the shopping centre on Friday evening along with everyone else, and queue an hour and a half to park, then another half hour to pay at the checkout. They could go to work in it, to their jobs that paid them large sums of money for doing totally insignificant things, until they retired to the garden of the house they were still buying back from the building society, to live on their pensions, and die from the heart attack bought on by all the years of stress and anxiety spent looking for parking space and wondering what was the point of their lives. Welcome to Suburbia, Michael thought.

Michael resigned himself to his fate and sat up. "Not in your case, no. They wouldn't give you a car in any case; your feet wouldn't touch the pedals."

"No . . ." Roland finished Michael's cornflakes, "I'm still gonna die young."

Michael snatched back the bowl that had meant to be his breakfast. "You won't starve to death, that's for sure!"

"I might go to Lebanon," Roland mused. "Become a suicide bomber."

"Islamic fundamentalism; you need to pass your RE for that."

"You need qualifications for everything these days."

"I know . . ." Michael threw off the blankets and reached for some clothes from the pile.

"Perhaps I should get a job advising the government?" said Roland, as Michael stepped into his shoes and grabbed his tie.

"No need," said Michael, "they've already got a load of idiots even dafter than you to do that for them; they're called the Civil Service."

Michael and Roland were inclined to conduct this kind of conversation when they were together. Nobody else could ever work out what they were talking about, and sometimes they couldn't either. They talked of new ways to save the world, arranging a spectacular death for Roland, and of how one day everyone in the world except them was going to be an estate agent or insurance salesman. They would be the mujihadeen of the home counties, laying ambushes for stray Yuppies on the North Downs. They each thought that the other was joking, but neither was sure.

Roland looked into the empty cornflake bowl: "I could do with some more food," he said.

"There you go," said June, bringing in the toast and Marmite.

The two boys were sitting at the dining table. Michael picked up the jar: "I don't have that muck!"

"It's not for you," said June, as Roland snatched the Marmite from him.

"Oh, don't mind me. I only live here!"

"There's your jam too," said June.

Michael and Roland sat eating the last of the cornflakes. Michael finished his and was going to reach for some toast, but he was too late. Roland was busily smothering all six slices in a mixture of Marmite and strawberry jam. Michael watched him fold one slice over, and stuff it in his mouth whole. Michael went to the kitchen.

Lin was in the kitchen dressed ready for school, putting some salad items into her lunchbox: "Well?" she said. "Are you going to ask her?"

"Ask who what?"

"Oh come on Micky. You said you liked her."

"Well there's no hurry, is there?"

"We'll go through it one more time, on the way to school."

"What about Sonny? I'm not having him taking the piss."

"Leave him to me," Lin said.

"Look, it's easy," she said, walking down the hill towards the school. "You just go up to her and say hello Treez . . ."

"How do I do that?"

"You open your mouth, and the words come out, Stupid!" Lin was beginning to lose her patience.

"What do I say after, then?" Michael really didn't have a clue.

"Oh, Micky!" Lin was exasperated, "how should I know?"

"Well you're the one that's telling me what to say."

Roland cautiously moved closer: "Have you finished yet?"

"No we haven't Sonny!" Lin shouted at him. "Get

46

back. This is private." Roland stood and let them walk ahead, like a naughty puppy who had been told to "stay". Roland had been a victim of Brownie attacks more than once, so he knew what was good for him.

"What if she doesn't want to be talked to?" Michael asked.

"She will," said Lin. "I told you. She likes you."

"Well what if she's already talking to someone else?"

"Micky, think of what Jimmy would do."

"He'd say, alright darlin', get your knickers off!"

"No he wouldn't."

"He'd think that," said Michael.

"He would not," said Lin, without much conviction.

"Oh yes he would," Michael insisted.

"Well whether he would or not, he doesn't say it."

"What does he say then? You'd know that."

Lin thought for a while: "He says nice things. He compliments you on how you look. Makes you feel like you're something special, like you were the only person in the world he wanted to talk to."

"So your advice is total dishonesty?"

"If you want to ask her," said Lin, "then you'll know what to say. It'll be whatever comes into your head."

"Hello Treez," said Michael, "isn't it funny how when someone offers you a fruit pastille, it's always a green one? Hello Treez, who do you think should be England's next wicket keeper? Hello Treez . . ."

Lin gave up: "You're just being stupid! As usual!"

"If all the Ford Sierras in the world were stuck on the M25 . . ." said Michael.

"Hello Treez," said James. "Get home alright?"

"Yes. Thanks." Theresa hung her coat up in the cloak-room area.

"I'm looking for a partner, for this afternoon."

Theresa assumed he meant for mixed badminton: "I don't expect you'll have any difficulty finding one," she said, not turning round.

"How about you?" He peered across her shoulder as he asked her. She was determined not to look at him.

"I'm with Lin." She turned her back to him again, and rearranged the books in her bag.

"OK," said James, "I'll get a partner for her, and between us we can hog a court all afternoon. Thanks for agreeing."

Agreeing? thought Theresa, who hadn't agreed to any-thing. She was going to tell him to hang on a minute, but when she turned around, he was gone.

Lin found Michael alone in a classroom at Breaktime. She made sure he came down to the Sixth Form Common Room, where she knew Theresa would be. "Now's your chance," she said. "Go on."

Theresa was sitting alone at the far corner of the Com-mon Room, reading. Michael stood at the entrance, looking in. Lin gave him a nudge, but his feet were nailed to the floor.

Lin sighed: "Alright, we'll do this together." She took his arm and led him smartly across the room. "You make a bolt for it now, Bigbruv," she said out of the corner of her mouth, "and I shall make sure everyone knows what a soppy great giant blackhead you are!"

Lin put Michael down on the seat next to Theresa, and sat herself on the opposite side of her.

"Treez." Lin made Theresa look up. "Micky's got lots he wants to talk to you about."

Theresa looked at Lin, and then at Michael. He said nothing, so she looked back to Lin, hoping for some explanation of what was going on.

"Micky wants to say hello." Lin smiled at Theresa, and then nodded at Michael. When Theresa turned to face Michael, Lin's smile quickly changed to an angry glare, aimed at her brother.

"Hello," said Michael, after a pause.

"Hello," said Theresa, speculating on the possibility of congenital mental illness in the Dobson family.

"Micky wants to ask you if you'll be playing badminton this afternoon," said Lin, continuing to prompt him.

"Does he?" Theresa asked, in a most doubtful voice.

"Yes," said Lin.

"Well why doesn't he?"

"He's going to."

"Is he?"

Lin nodded vigorously at Michael.

"You playing badminton this afternoon?" he said.

Theresa turned back to Lin: "He's very good," she said. "Did you teach him to talk yourself?"

Lin's heart sank. Why was it, she wondered, that when most of the time it was impossible for her to shut him up, now she couldn't get him to say a word. All Michael did was go very red.

"OK," Theresa said.

"OK?" Lin was not quite sure she had heard right.

Theresa looked at the clock, and put away her book. She stood up, and edged past Lin to leave: "I'll see you later," she said to her.

"Alright," said Lin.

Theresa left. Lin looked in disbelief at Michael.

49

"This chatting girls up lark," he said, "quite easy really, isn't it?"

At lunchtime, James, Michael and Roland made their way out of the school playground, through the uniformed ranks of the younger ones.

"Hello Jimmy." An angel-faced Fourth Year girl called to him, her friends all giggling around her. James gave her a wink, and they giggled some more.

"Bit too old for you, I'd say," said Michael.

"Hey! Sonny!" Some small boys shouted to Roland. He gave them the thumbs up.

"Part of your Dwarf Army?" asked Michael.

"Where's your fan club then, Mike?"

"Well I've got you two following me home," he told James. They passed the school gates, and walked up the hill to Michael's house.

Lunch was always a welcome hour's refuge from the tiresome grind of school. The boys had it well organised. Michael did the cooking, James did the washing up and Roland scoffed most of the food.

"Is it ready yet?" Roland shouted from the living room.

"Ah, shut up," cried Michael from the kitchen, poking expertly under the grill with a fork. Satisfied that all was ready, he removed the sausages from the heat, and carefully cut them and placed them on the bread.

"Can I put another record on, Mike?"

"So long as it's not any of your funky-boogie stuff," called Michael, arranging the sausages in the sandwiches.

"No, it's some of your pretentious-meaningful stuff." James leafed through the selection. He chose a record and put it on.

Michael brought in the food, and handed out the plates.

"Mike, you'll make someone a wonderful wife one day."

"Big game this afternoon," Roland said, drowning a sausage sandwich in tomato sauce.

"You mean your showdown with the Fifth Years?" James said. "Count me out."

"No problem," said Roland. "We need footballers, not posers, eh Micky?"

"I shan't be playing."

"What d'you mean?" Roland demanded. "You always play."

"I shall be inside," Michael announced, "posing with him."

Roland was aghast. "What? Shuttlecocks? You?"

"It's a game of skill and balance," said James.

Roland could think of another reason: "It's an excuse to get in with the girlies."

"That too," said James.

School Games had been invented, Michael thought, partly in an effort to get the scrawny half-starved pre-war kids fit, and partly to take their dirty little minds off each others bodies with five mile runs and cold showers and stuff. Now with the welfare state and co-education, once a week a large horde of smouldering overgrown adolescence took most of its clothes off and crammed into the Sports Hall together to gawp and gape. Progress, Michael thought.

"When they lean forward to receive service," said Roland, "you can see right down their fronts."

"I would have thought you'd need a step ladder for that," Michael suggested.

"No, he's just right for it," said James. "Remember that time he bumped into Chesty Cheryl in the corridor? What a way to get a nosebleed."

"Better than a boot up the bum anyday," said Roland.

"You'll get plenty of those this afternoon," Michael predicted.

James turned to Michael: "Got yourself a partner?"

"Yeah."

"Who is it?"

"Well, it't not you."

"Just as well. I only play mixed doubles."

"We'll give you a game," Michael offered.

Now it was James's turn to be astonished: "You mean you managed to get a girl for a partner? I wondered why you weren't playing football. Who is it?"

"Just someone I asked at Break," Michael said, nonchalantly.

"It's not your sister, is it?" James asked.

"No," said Michael, "and it's not yours either."

"Well. We'll give you a game then?"

"Alright."

"Pouffy bleeding shuttlecocks, I don't know," said Roland, contemptuously.

"But women don't play football, Sonny," said James.

"One, two, three!" said Jill, standing on one of the changing room benches.

"Here we go, here we go, here we go!" A chorus of girls shouted. The hockey team were in their usual appalling voice, ready for the match against the girls from Our Lady The Virgin.

"I suppose if you're losing, you could always sing to them," Theresa suggested.

"We won't lose," said Jill. "We cheat better than they do."

"And we've got our secret weapons," said Clare.

"Secret weapons?" said Lin, folding her school jumper. "You're dangerous enough with those sticks, aren't you? Especially her," she said, meaning Jill Bryce.

"Our secret weapons," said Clare, "are our cheerleader . . ." Up stepped Zahira, not allowed by the school to play hockey in her tracksuit, and not allowed by her father to play in a skirt. She was looking very pleased with herself and waving two very large pom-poms: "Yea!" shouted the hockey team.

"And also our spy," said Clare. There was another cheer, and Paula O'Leary, recent escapee from Our Lady, gave a curtsey.

"Polly's told us which ones to mark," Jill explained.

"And which ones to put in hospital," Clare added.

"We'd better be getting down to the field," said Jill.

"O.K. See you," said Lin.

"Have fun with the fellahs in the Sports Hall," said Clare, rousing a lewd chorus from the rest of the hockey girls. They marched out of the changing room, Zahira leading the way with her two giant powder-puffs, Jill conducting the caterwauling: "Here we go, here we go, here we go!"

Lin tied up her shoes, and was ready to move, but Theresa, as ever, was taking twice as long.

"So Jimmy reckons he's partnering you?" said Lin, waiting for Theresa to get herself organised.

"That's right." Theresa poked her head through the neck of her tennis shirt, nearly knocking the glasses off her nose. "But he reckons wrong."

"I wondered why you agreed when Micky asked. Didn't think you fell for his smooth talk."

"Not exactly, no."

"Micky's shy," Lin explained. "Normally he's ever so funny."

Theresa pulled up her tracksuit trousers. "He certainly

seemed pretty strange this morning." She looked at Lin's old green school games skirt, now a very tight fit. "I don't know how you can still wear that thing."

"It's alright," said Lin, blandly.

"In front of all those lecherous boys?"

"More on show at the swimming baths." Lin was quite unconcerned as ever. "We'll have to move quickly if we're going to get a court."

"I'd rather not go out there yet. Not till the footballers have gone outside."

"You don't want to worry about them."

"Oh come on," said Theresa, "have you heard some of the things they call out when you walk past them?"

"It's the quiet ones you want to watch out for," said Lin. "The ones that stand in narrow doorways, so that you have to brush against them when you go past."

"I know about them, that's what the racquet's for." Theresa demonstrated its use as an offensive weapon.

"What about the ones that lie on the floor by the side of the court? I hate them."

"It's pathetic, isn't it? You'd think they'd have grown out of that one by now," Theresa demonstrated a shot: "Misdirected smash in the eye," she said.

"Can you do that?"

"Sometimes. They get the message, at any rate."

"You play this game all the time," said Lin. "How come?"

"Not a lot of choice when you're as short-sighted as I am," Theresa explained. "Wrong time of year for tennis. I can't play hockey, and they won't let me on the trampoline in tracksuit bottoms."

"So take them off," Lin suggested. "Wear shorts, or do it in your knickers, like we used to have to." Theresa gave Lin a cold stare. "Sorry," said Lin.

"I'd like to go swimming sometime," said Theresa, "but you know what happens there, don't you?"

Lin nodded sympathetically. "Speaking of lechers, what are we going to do about Jimmy?"

"Ah. That's where I was hoping you might help me out."

"Help you? I thought you had a shot for every occasion?"

"Oh please Lin."

"Alright, but only if you promise to come back for tea this afternoon, and talk to Micky." Theresa sighed, but Lin persisted. "He's ever so nice really, when you know him properly. Come on, you don't have to stay long."

"I haven't got the time," Theresa claimed. "I want to get down the library this afternoon. I want to get a book on self-defence."

Theresa was not going to get caught out again like she was the other night. She had seen an article somewhere about assertiveness. That was what she needed, she had decided. Facing up to Lin, she could have done with some right away.

"I reckon you must live in that library," said Lin. "Well, if you're going to be like that, I might as well go and join Zed down at the hockey."

"What? And miss the chance of partnering Jimmy?"

"I don't know what you mean by that?" Lin pretended not to understand, but without much conviction.

"I'll come," said Theresa, resignedly, "for a cup of tea, nothing else. Then I'm off."

"Down the library, I know," said Lin. "Listen, this is what we're going to do."

"Jimmy!" Lin bounced up to him. "It's Treez, she wants to see you."

"What's the matter?"

"She says sorry, but she can't join you."

"Why not?"

"She's hurt her leg. It's ever so sore," she said. "She wants you to come and see, to prove she's not making it up. She's down by the lockers."

James strode off in the direction of the lockers, speculating on his chances of offering a massage.

Michael approached Lin. "What's up?"

"Just do as you're told, Bigbruv." Lin waved, and Theresa appeared through the doors. "You two get on a court," she said, "I've got to go and find Jimmy."

"What's she up to?" Michael asked.

Theresa occupied the last free court. "Just play," she said, offering him service.

"Where's she gone?" James was standing between the lockers looking lost.

"Ah," said Lin. "I sort of lied, a bit."

James looked out into the Sports Hall, and saw Theresa and Michael on court together. "Oh, I get it." He poked Lin in the stomach with his racquet. "You're up to your tricks again, aren't you?"

She fended him off. "You're the one that plays tricks. Treez says she never agreed to partner you."

James protested. "I can't stand around all day waiting for a yes or no. It's not my fault if she can't come out with a straight refusal."

"She says you never gave her the chance to refuse, and she wants to partner Micky."

She faced right up to him. Her eyes came up level with his neck. "OK. Have it your way," he said.

"So you'll leave her alone from now on?"

"Plenty more fishes in the sea."

"Since when were you interested in fish?"

"What's that supposed to mean?"

"You know," Lin told him. "You were practically drooling, just now."

He pulled away from her. "I'm only playing this stupid game because of her. I should be resting my shoulder, really."

Lin looked at him suspiciously. "There's nothing wrong with your shoulder."

"Isn't there?" He lifted his shirt over his head, and revealed a large ugly bruise. "What about that then?"

She came closer. "Ooh, it's horrible. How did you get it?"

"Fell off the bike, on the way home from school the other day."

"Does it hurt?" She ran her finger to the centre of the mark, making him flinch. "Oh sorry."

"No, it's alright," he said. "Just don't poke it, that's all."

"That better?" She stroked his back very gently.

James flexed his shoulders in satisfaction. He began to laugh. "You fell for that one, didn't you?"

"Pig!" She slapped him hard. He laughed some more, and tried to grab her arms. She poked him hard in the middle of his bruise, and he let go, reaching for his wound. "I hope it goes septic and your arm drops off!"

"You any good at this game?" James asked, pulling his shirt back on.

"Rotten."

"Well I'm brilliant," said James, "except I've got this bad shoulder, see."

James left Theresa's lob, but it landed on the line. "In!" shouted Michael.

"Game to you," said James.

"Can we have a break?" asked Lin, worn out.

Leaving the court would mean losing it, so the two pairs sat down on opposite sides of the net.

"You're pretty good."

James would surely have made something of that remark, but Michael realised she was talking badminton. "Not as good as you," he said.

"Well I've probably had more practice. Do you mind if I give you a couple of tips?"

"No." Michael shrugged his shoulders.

"Well, first of all, when you smash; aim it right in their faces."

Michael nodded: "I like the sound of that."

"And when I'm at the back of the court and I shout for you to leave," she continued, "you duck, or you might get it in the back of the head."

"I never realised this was such a violent game."

"It's even better when you play it with conkers instead of shuttlecocks."

"Why aren't you out playing hockey with the rest of the homicidal maniacs?"

"Left-handed," Theresa explained.

"Same here."

"That's why we make such a good pair. We don't get in each other's way."

"Plus, I bet, you can't see the ball in hockey without those?" Michael suggested.

"I can't see the field without these," she said. "Shall we murder them a third time?"

"Yeah, but can I give you a tip first?"

"What's that?"

"Do that button up." Michael pointed at Theresa's collar with his racquet, "when you lean forward, he has a good look."

"Thanks." Theresa fastened the button. She had never thought of that one. They both stood up.

"Your serve." Michael threw a shuttle back over the net. Lin served, Theresa shouted "leave", and smashed it back; right into James's eye. Michael exchanged a knowing glance with Theresa as he rose to his feet. "Service over." James tossed the shuttle back over the net. "There's no need to take it so seriously!"

Michael served. Lin put up a weak return, and Theresa buried it to win the point. "It's a game of skill and balance, Jimbo," Michael called.

It wasn't long before Theresa was serving for the match. After a couple of returns, James's attempted smash landed out. Michael and Theresa both lifted their arms in triumph. She stepped forward towards him, and patted him on the back: "Well done," she said.

Feeling her hand on his back, Michael froze for an instant before reaching out to return the compliment. By that time, though, she was on the move again. He just managed to lay half a hand on her before she was at the net, talking to James and Lin.

"Aren't you supposed to jump over to our side now?" asked James.

"I'd need the trampoline for that," she said.

James looked across the hall to where a girl was bouncing almost to the roof. For him, badminton had completely lost its appeal.

"I think we're going to have to get off now," said Lin. "There's people been waiting to get a game."

"I could do with a rest," Theresa agreed.

When Michael finally approached the net, the girls were already walking off.

"Listen Mike, I'll see you in a while, OK." James strolled off in the direction of the trampoline. Michael was left standing on his own, with four impatient girls glaring at him, waiting for him to clear the court. He saw James climb onto the trampoline, and in no time he and the girl were holding hands, bouncing higher and higher. He cleared the court and the badminton girls started to knock up. One of them had legs so smooth they reflected the sunlight coming through the roof. Michael went to get a drink of water.

Michael found Roland sitting on the floor by the lockers, bouncing a football against the wall opposite. "What are you doing down there?"

"Nothing," said Roland.

"Well why aren't you out playing football?"

"Only five people turned up."

"Where have they all gone, then?"

"Down the field. They all wanted to watch the hockey."

"Spectator blood sport," said Michael. "Why didn't you go with them?"

"Nah," said Roland. "I get enough of that at home. Football's no good anymore, anyway."

"It's because most people who played in our games left after the Fifth Year," Michael recalled. "Remember our non-stop matches? What was the record score?"

"241-209," said Roland. "I scored 88 goals."

"With another fifty-odd disallowed," Michael reminded him.

In those days, the boys used to get to school half an

hour early to start the game in the playground. They used to play all through Break and Lunchtime. Michael was a midfield ball-player, Roland was a busy little goalscorer and the only stoppages were for the lessons that, so annoyingly, kept interrupting the run of play. After school, when everyone else had gone home, Roland, Michael and a few friends often used to stay behind, kicking a ball against the side of the Sports Hall until it got too dark to see. Football-Squash, it was called; there was also Football-Tennis (when the nets were set up), Football-Golf (all around the playground drain-covers), and Football-Polo (on bicycles). Life was football, television and the top 20. The world outside the school gates was a strange and threatening place, and French lessons were strictly for thinking up silly sketches and picking the latest England squad.

"Come on," said Michael, "I'll give you a game of something."

Theresa and Lin had climbed to the top of the apparatus in search of somewhere to sit undisturbed. From there, they watched all the goings on below, including James, who was now giving a piggy-back ride to the girl from off the trampoline: "Nothing wrong with his shoulder now," said Lin.

"What's that?"

"Nothing."

"Where's Micky gone?" asked Theresa.

"I don't know." Lin sounded suddenly eager. "Shall we go look for him?"

"No," Theresa said, irritated. "I just asked."

"But you like him though, don't you?"

Theresa drew breath. "What do you mean by like?"

61

"Like," repeated Lin. "Opposite of dislike."

"Yes, I like him," admitted Theresa.

"Interested in, want to get to know better . . ." continued Lin.

Theresa paused for a moment to reflect. "Yes," she admitted.

"Just can't wait to stick your slobbery tongue in his earhole and wiggle it around?" suggested Lin, mischievously.

"Shut up, you!" Theresa nudged Lin with her elbow.

"Ah," said Lin, gleefully, "you don't deny it then?"

"Lin, how would you like to practise your high diving?" Theresa pushed Lin, in an effort to dislodge her from her perch. Lin pushed back, they both nearly fell, and ended up clinging onto each other for dear life, giggling like a pair of little kids.

James, Michael and Roland always managed to disappear to the changing room five minutes early. That way they missed the crowds, and avoided having to help pack away any equipment.

"Who won the shuttlecocks, then?" asked Roland.

"We did," Michael reported. "No contest."

"I might have a go at shuttlecocks next week." Roland played a couple of ridiculous air shots.

"You'd need to get a pair of stilts first," Michael told him. "You coming round to steal what's left of our food then?"

"If you insist," he said.

"How about you Jim? You coming round?"

James emerged from out of the shower, rubbing himself with a towel. "No thanks, I've got a driving lesson." He sat down with the towel in his lap, and reached into his bag for his roll-on.

Roland found this highly amusing. "Deodorant. For Men!" he growled, in a deep voice. James ignored him.

Michael put on his school trousers over his football shorts, while Roland stuffed all his school clothes, jacket and all, into his bag and zipped it up.

"Don't you two ever wash then?" said James, standing up and pulling on his briefs.

"Wash?" said Roland, quizzically, as if he'd never heard the word before.

"Pay no attention to him Sonny, washing's got nothing to do with what he's up to."

"What are you talking about?" James stared at the pair of them. They both stared back at him, standing there in only his underwear.

"It's alright, I understand," Michael assured James. "You feel this need, this urge, to exhibit yourself."

"What are you going on about?" James had never been able to figure out what the two of them thought they had to hide.

"Exhibitionism," said Michael, "it's a well known psychological disorder. Most of them start like you."

"Them? Who's Them?" asked James.

"Dirty Old Men," said Michael. "Flashers."

"Perverts," added Roland.

"Come on Sonny, we'd better not stay in here alone with him."

"Urrrrrgh," said Roland, snatching his bag and backing away from a bemused James. They left him on his own.

Outside the changing rooms, there was a crush of bodies in mud-splashed kit back from the field. Theresa and Lin were carried in by the tide. All around them the hockey team fell in, with shouts of "champions" and "six-one".

"Was that the score, or the casualty list?" asked Theresa.

"The score! We murdered 'em," said Jill.

"Is that water hot?" Clare was wrapped in a towel, waiting to go into the shower. A shout from behind the splash screen said that it was.

"Wait a minute!" Paula called, "I think there's two boys out there, trying to peek in."

"Where are they?" Lin hastily zipped up her school skirt.

"Leaning against the radiator," said Paula. "When the door opens, they can see right across that side of the room."

Lin stepped into the danger zone, and waited for someone else to come through the door. If it was Jimmy out there, she thought, she would give him a lot more than a sore shoulder. The door opened. Lin caught a brief glimpse of two well-known Lower Sixth pests, neither of them friends of hers. They both leaned forward as the door swung shut. "Yes, they're out there," she said.

"We should report them to Mrs Garrett," Theresa suggested, meaning the deputy head in charge of Sixth Form.

"That old cow won't do anything about it," said Clare.

Brownie Girls did not go to teachers with their problems. Jill Bryce picked up her hockey stick: "Looks like a girl's gotta do what a girl's gotta do," she said. "I shan't be long."

"I'm coming with you," said Paula, brandishing her stick like a Samurai sword.

When the two girls went out, behind them the whole changing room moved up to the door to listen to what happened next. Those near the front of the crowd could hear several cries, the last two sounding particularly loud and painful. The two girls re-entered the changing room, surrounded by the crowd eager to hear the details.

"They won't try that again," said Paula, looking pleased with herself.

"No, from now on they'll be singing in the choir," said Jill. Everyone laughed.

The Brownie Girls formed a ring, and placed their hands in the centre of it: "Through thick and thin, through stormy weather, Brownie Girls stick together!" they shouted. *Stick* together indeed, Theresa thought.

Clare ran into the shower, and screamed: "Aaah! You never said it was that hot."

"Stop complaining," Jill called out. "It's good for you."

"You think so? You try it!"

"I'm just coming!" Jill kicked her shoes off. "Watch that door for me, someone."

"Right." Theresa stepped over to stand guard.

"Did you see that film?" said Jill. "The one where those boys made a hole in the wall, so's they could watch the girls in the shower?"

"I know the one you mean," said Theresa. "Not my idea of a good film."

"No, didn't think it would be," said Jill.

"No Polish subtitles," Lin explained.

"Well I saw it," Jill told them, "and I thought it was funny at the time. Not any more."

"It's a form of violence," said Theresa, articulating Jill's feelings. "A non-physical assault."

"They just don't realise," said Lin.

"Well they should be made to realise," said Jill, disappearing into the steam.

"Polly and Jill gave those two out there something to think about," said Lin.

"Does it have to come to that? That we have to arm ourselves, and keep lookouts all the time?" Theresa asked.

"They're not all like that," said Lin. "Thank God."

"No," Theresa agreed.

"Shame they don't wear badges so you can tell which ones are," Paula suggested.

"My name is so and so, and I am a pig," Theresa proposed.

"Before you find your prince, you have to kiss a load of frogs," said Lin.

"And pigs," said Theresa, "if you're not careful."

"And rats," added Paula.

"Forget the Disco," Jill shouted from behind the screen, "let's all go down the zoo."

"They're the ones that call us dogs," said Theresa. "Remember?"

"Have you finished that drawing yet?" Michael asked, as he and Roland walked up the hill together.

"Might have done."

"Well show us it then. Please?"

Roland halted, and fought his way into his bag. Throwing out various items of clothing onto the pavement, he eventually found his sketchpad. The drawing was an alternative version of the official Sixth Form boys' photo.

"Oh yes, love it," said Michael. "Who's that?"

"Who?"

"That idiot there."

Roland looked closely. "What? The really stupid looking one?"

"Yeah."

"That's you."

"No it's not, there's me," Michael said. "Where's Jim?"

"That one." Roland pointed. Michael laughed. "Hang on . . ." Roland pulled out a pen, "he's not finished."

"What you doing?"

"Putting in the vapours from his after-shave."

"I'm going to draw you." Michael snatched the pen from Roland.

"Get off!" Roland fought Michael for control of the paper. "You'll ruin it, you will."

"Oh look, Treez, the children are fighting in the street," said Lin, as they caught up with the two boys.

"There you are," said Michael. "Finished."

"You have completely buggered my masterpiece," cried Roland.

"What is it?" Theresa asked. Michael snatched the drawing from Roland and handed it to her: "It's very good," she said to Michael. "Can I photocopy it?"

"Ask Sonny, it's his picture."

"Can I borrow it please, Sonny?"

"Have it," said Roland. "It's not worth anything, not now it's been vandalised."

"Don't be silly, it's really good."

Theresa tried to be friendly, but Roland seemed unwilling to talk to her. "I'd better be going," he said.

"But you said you were coming round," Michael protested, but to no effect. Roland stuffed everything back into his bag, and headed off to the bus stop, without pausing to say goodbye.

"What did I do?" Theresa was mystified.

"Oh never mind him," said Lin, "he's always acting funny." In fact, Lin was delighted that Roland would not now be around. It would be much easier for her to get Michael and Theresa alone together. "Come on," she said. "I'm making the tea."

"There's something the matter with Sonny," Michael said to Lin in the kitchen.

"You've just noticed, have you?"

"No, I mean something bothering him, I reckon."

"Well don't let it bother you now. You just get talking to her. I'll come in in a minute to see how you're getting on, and if you're doing alright, I'll disappear upstairs."

When Michael brought the tea in, Theresa was studying Roland's cartoon. "They ought to put this in the school magazine," she said.

"I doubt it," Michael told her.

"Why not?"

"Sonny got thrown out of Art last year," he revealed, "for drawing obscene pictures of the Head and Mrs Garrett."

"Obscene?"

"Well, not obscene, no, but they weren't very flattering."

"And so they didn't let him take his exam? That's rotten."

"They were just looking for an excuse to chuck him out," Michael told her. "It's a wonder they ever let him come back for another year."

"He should do one of the girls as well," she said. "I've got the photo."

"We've got the photo." Michael opened a drawer in the bureau. "Here it is, in with the rest of them."

He handed the album of school photos to Theresa. She sat on the sofa looking at them. Michael sat down next to her to go through the pages together. "Oh look at you both," she said, holding up the picture of Michael and Lin as 1st and 2nd Years, competing with each other to show the greatest area of teeth.

"The only time they could get him to pose with me," said Lin, entering.

"Well, you were such a nice little girl then. All those years ago."

"Show her the one of you when you had long hair," said Lin. Theresa smiled at the sight of Michael the Fourth Year Hippy.

"There's some terrible ones of me at home," Theresa confessed.

"What about when you had the plaits?" Lin grabbed Theresa's hair at the sides, "and those stupid specs you always wore then?"

"Ugh, don't remind me," said Theresa, fending her off.

"Do you remember that, Micky?" Lin asked.

"I can't remember Micky ever being in when I used to come round," said Theresa.

"No, I used to run out of the house whenever your gang invaded," Michael told her.

"Remember when we chased him out? When we said we all wanted to kiss him?"

"No, I must have missed that one," said Theresa.

"I bet you wouldn't run away now, eh Micky?"

"I would if it was you."

"Don't give me that," said Lin. "I know you love me really." She stood up: "I'm going upstairs to change. I won't be too long." She shut the door behind her.

Theresa looked at Michael sat next to her on the sofa. She had been enjoying the conversation, but now she was struck dumb with embarrassment.

"She's not very subtle, my Sis."

Theresa was relieved that he was aware of the situation: "She's been planning this for days."

Michael gave a smirk, and immediately wished he hadn't. He didn't know what to say.

Theresa felt uneasy. Her mouth had gone dry. She gulped some tea and it went down the wrong way. She choked.

69

"Lin's tea has that effect on most people," said Michael, nervously, trying to make a joke.

Theresa carried on choking, bent forward as though she were going to be sick. Not sure what to do, Michael leant across and slapped her on the back. She stopped. She took a couple of breaths and sat back up. Michael looked at her anxiously to see if she was alright. Theresa looked back at Michael, worried that she was making such a scene. Sensing the absurdity of the situation, both of them broke into awkward little smiles. It was then that they both became aware of how close they were sitting, and that Michael still had his hand on the middle of Theresa's back. Theresa's lower jaw slowly opened. Have you got any more photos? she was going to ask, and he would have to move. But the words wouldn't come out. "I've got to go," she mumbled, and made a bolt for the door.

When Lin came down the stairs, Theresa was putting her coat on.

"What's the matter?"

"I can't stay. I've got to get to the library. I've got this essay to do, for next week ... Oh Lin I'm sorry about this ..."

"Has Micky tried to do anything with you?"

"Oh no," said Theresa, "nothing."

"No." Lin sounded almost disappointed. "Didn't think he would."

"It's not Micky's fault." Theresa was repeatedly missing the buttonholes on her coat, "it's just that I don't, I mean I ... Oh ... Thanks for the tea."

Lin found Michael hovering inside the doorway. "Well

don't just stand there like some dummy in a shop window, go and speak to her!" She pushed him out into the hall.

"Treez."

"I'm sorry about this Micky."

"S'alright. I hate girls who won't let go of me until they've had their way with me. You make a nice change."

He hadn't done or said anything to justify this, thought Theresa, he must have been just as nervous as she was. And yes, she did like him a lot. "Can I talk to you tomorrow?" she asked. "Somewhere private."

"Private?"

"Somewhere away from Lin."

He knew exactly what she meant. "I know a place."

"Tell Sonny I'll give him his sketch back tomorrow," she promised.

"I will."

She opened the door.

"Will you be playing pouffy shuttlecocks next week?" Michael said, holding the door.

"What's that?"

"It's Sonny's name for badminton."

"Oh, yes I am. How about you?"

"Mmm."

"Do you want to carry on the partnership?"

"Yes. Thanks."

"See you tomorrow in school then?"

"OK," he said.

"Bye then."

"Bye." Michael saw her out, then shut the door behind her.

Lin came out into the hall when she heard the door shut. "Well?" she said.

"Well what?"

"What did she say?"

"I'm seeing her tomorrow in school."

Lin went mad. "Oh that's great! Oh Micky, I knew you could do it! You sexy beast you!"

"Get off me, you stupid daft cow!" he said, pushing her away.

"I told you she really likes you." Lin was already planning ahead. "Now your next move," she said, following him upstairs, "is the school disco on Friday. I'll make sure Treez comes, so you won't have to invite her."

"School disco? Do me a favour Lin."

"Oh come on, you'll like it."

"I won't."

"You will."

"Bloody won't," said Michael.

"How do you know? You've never even been to a Sixth Form bop."

"And I never will, with any luck."

"Well you're out of luck aren't you, because you're coming." She had made her mind up.

Lin followed Michael up and down stairs, in and out of rooms, detailing how she was going to make him ready for the big night. He tried to fight her off, but it was no use. She was like a kitten chasing a ball of wool, and there was no losing Lin once she had her claws dug into something.

"I'll do your hair for you . . ."

"You are not touching my hair!"

"It needs washing."

"I can wash my own hair, can't I!"

"You don't wash it properly," she said. "And you'll have to borrow some of Dad's deodorant."

Michael had been pushed too far. "I am not wearing deodorant!" he said.

Chapter 3

Friday morning period 2 in the Sixth Form Study Room was not the best place to attempt any serious study. In most people's books, the weekend had already begun. James, Michael and Roland had managed to find a space, though, and it was Roland, of all people, who was keen to get some work done.

"How do you find the angle on these?" Roland asked, struggling with his Maths.

"You use a calculator," said Michael, unhelpfully.

"I know that," Roland said, "but which of the buttons are you meant to push?"

"I don't know what's the matter with you today, Sonny," said James. "I thought you were in training for the British Olympic skiving team?"

"It's my day off," Roland explained, although it might also have had something to do with the imminent approach of Lower Sixth mock exams. He leafed through the pages of his maths textbook with a look of glazed incomprehension. He continued to wrestle with his triangles, books, paper and folders strewn across the desk, but his concentration was abruptly disturbed by the arrival on his desk of a large and, to him, most unattractive item.

It was a backside, belonging to Tim Taylor of the Upper Sixth. Tim had decided to make an early start on his weekend homework, a serious and highly detailed study of all aspects of Tracy Latimer of the Lower Sixth. Roland threw down his pen in dispair.

Michael was busy reading a football magazine. He looked

up to see what was happening. "She'd put him down if she knew where he's been."

Roland shifted his books, and attempted to carry on working. It wasn't long though, before he was interrupted again. First, a shadow began to obscure his view, then, a black-stockinged leg shot across the front of his face, very nearly knocking his front teeth out: "Gordon Bennett! Aren't there places people can go to do this?" he demanded.

"There's teachers patrolling all the cloakrooms for smokers," said James.

"And the caretaker gets his kicks from peering behind the Sports Hall," Michael added.

"But there must be a more comfortable place for a snog than here," Roland complained.

"There's the Art block storeroom," James suggested.

"But that's reserved for certain illegal activities," said Michael.

"You mean funny fags?"

"Funny fags? I don't know anything at all about funny fags," said Michael. "Do you know anything about funny fags, Jim?"

"Absolutely nothing." James vigorously shook his head. In fact, everyone knew about the school's select little band of grass-smokers; everyone except a few complete dimwits and the occasional deputy headteacher.

Roland was being pushed more and more into the corner by the disturbance on the table. In an effort to gain more space, he took hold of the offending leg, swung it back across to the other side of the table, and pulled one of Tim's hands down to support it, thus removing any further risk to himself of decapitation.

Lin marched into the centre of the room. "Disco tickets," she called out. A crowd quickly gathered around her.

"No tickets on the door, so this could be your last chance. Mrs Garrett says no alcohol allowed in school tonight, so nobody's going to bring any drink, are they?"

There was much shaking of heads and audible denials from all around. Tonight, the litter bins outside the school would be bulging with empty bottles and cans. Large amounts of alcohol would be brought into school, but The Head of Sixth Form would need a stomach pump to get at it.

Lin continued: "I shall be around with tickets at Break and Lunch, so anyone who wants one can get if off me." There was a lewd cheer. "A ticket," she repeated. Speech over, Lin made her way around the Study Room, cajoling as many people as possible to come along. Eventually, she came to the boys. "Disco tickets," she called. Tim Taylor reached into his pocket, took out some money and bought two tickets, without ever letting go of Tracy Latimer.

"Can I have two please, Lin?" James asked.

Lin handed him his tickets. "Didn't think you'd be coming on your own. There you are," she said, "one for you, and one for your latest love; Louise Foreman, 5B3, isn't it?"

Lin looked as if she wasn't very pleased with James's choice. James was slightly taken aback. "Who told you?"

"My spies are everywhere."

"I bet they are," James said.

"You can do better than her, you know," said Lin, meaning herself. "I heard she changes her boyfriends more often than her knickers, that one."

"You're worse than the KGB, you are," James protested.

"It's not the KGB, it's the Brownie Pack. Now, Micky . . ." She turned to her brother, "I've got a couple of tickets stashed away for you both, you can give me the money later."

"Look, who says I'm coming?" Michael demanded. "Who says she's coming?"

"Oh stop being stupid. You'll love it, both of you."

"Oh yes?" James turned to Michael. "You trying your luck as well tonight, are you?"

"Pardon?"

"Reckon you'll be well in with Treez, do you?"

"Go and buy your girlfriend a lollipop, Jim. She'd like that."

"Why don't you go and get yours a book token?" James suggested. "That would really turn her on."

"She is not my girlfriend, OK?"

Roland spoke. "I want a ticket."

"You?" said Lin.

"Him?" said James.

"Me," said Roland. "I fancy a boogie."

"Now that, I have got to see," said James.

"Just one problem," said Roland.

"What's that?" Lin asked.

"I know what," said Michael.

"Haven't got any money," said Roland, looking forlorn.

"No problem." James dug into his pocket for change. "You're better than a couple of drinks anyday."

"Oh great," said Lin, "that means nearly everyone's coming."

"Who says I'm coming?" Michael repeated.

"Oh stop it Micky!" Lin said. "I'll talk to Treez, don't worry."

"I'm having a word with her, in a minute," Michael said. "On my own."

"On your own, eh?" James said it suggestively.

"Yes," said Michael, "a private talk."

"I've never heard it called that before," said James.

"I don't expect you have, Jim. No."

It was nearly time for the bell to go, and Michael got up to leave. Tim Taylor and Tracy Latimer carried on, completely oblivious to whatever else might have been happening around them.

James pointed to the unwelcome guests on Roland's table. "I hope you've been paying attention to this, Mike, so you know what to do."

Michael waited for Theresa outside her English class, and then led her out of the school and across to the playing fields. They sat on one of the park benches. It was a cold, grey and gusty day, so no one with any sense was about.

Michael pulled up the collar of his jacket against the wind. "Nice day for a walk."

Theresa was only wearing her school pullover. "Surprising there aren't more people out enjoying the sunshine," she said, shivering. "Sorry about yesterday afternoon."

"S'alright," said Michael.

"Lin seems to have got the wrong idea. She's got it into her head that I'm, well, keen on you, and that's not the case."

"Thanks a bunch! I hate you too."

"No, I didn't mean it like that, Micky. I mean I do like you, as a person. Oh, that sounds daft, doesn't it?"

Michael put on a silly voice. "I like you as a person, but not as a chest of drawers. Yes, it does sound daft."

"Well all the words are wrong, aren't they? A boy friend sounds like a 'Boyfriend'. You can't so much as say hello to someone of the opposite sex without rumours starting to circulate."

"I know what you mean," he said, "and they circulate fast, thanks to certain people we could mention."

Theresa mentioned a certain person. "Lin's been pestering me all morning to go to this disco tonight."

"Me too," said Michael.

"She thinks Cupid's little arrows will work their magic on us. She means well, but she can be a right pain, sometimes."

"You should try living with her."

"I expect she'll send her Stormtroopers round to collect me tonight."

"Well, set the dog on 'em," Michael suggested.

"Too cruel. She'd lick them to death."

"What are you going to do then?" Michael was nearly choking, hoping that she would say that she was coming.

"I suppose I'll have to come," she said. "How about you?"

"It's no use fighting Lin. When an idea penetrates its way into her skull, it stays there. Good job it doesn't happen very often, really." Yes, he thought. Yes, she is coming. Good. Great. Fantastic!

Theresa returned to her point: "So if you say you like someone, someone of a dissimilar gender, shall we say?"

"Someone of the alternative chromosome pattern," Michael suggested. "Someone whose buttons do up the other way around."

"That's it." Theresa concurred. "If you do express an interest, then it is automatically assumed that you are after the usual biology practical."

"And if you're not, then you ought to be."

"If you're not, then there's something wrong with you," she said, "you've committed the ultimate crime of not being exactly the same as everybody else."

"What I can't stand," Michael said, "is that if you're a boy, it's not even enough to be interested in sex; you're supposed to be obsessed by it every minute of the day, otherwise you're suspect."

"You should try being a girl," she told him, "then you'd have to choose between being called frigid or a slag. Me? I'm Miss Concrete Knickers of the Sixth Form, in case you didn't know."

"Stick with me, kid, and you'll get a much better class of personal abuse than that." Michael wanted to say something serious. "Look, Treez, will you promise me something?"

"What?"

It was no good. Serious was just too difficult, he thought. "Well, I like you too . . . as a person. Promise me you won't turn into a pound of rhubarb or anything?"

"I promise."

"Big deal. All the girls say that."

"I'm not All The Girls."

"Good job too, or there wouldn't be enough room for you on this bench, would there?"

"So, if Lin expects us to finish up snogging in the cloakroom, she's going to be out of luck, isn't she?"

"Is she?" Michael told himself over and over that he was interested in Theresa for all sorts of reasons, and he was. It was just that one reason kept jumping up and down in his mind again and again. He wished it would go away. Alright, perhaps he didn't, really.

"Yes!" Theresa was beginning to get quite irate. "And so are you, by the look of things." Theresa thought sex with a boy sounded like an extremely good idea in theory, it was just the loathsome spotty offensive articles found in practice who were so completely unimpressive. Michael seemed different, some of the time, but at other times he seemed the same as all the others. She didn't know what to make of him, yet, except that he almost certainly stood no chance. Well, perhaps he did, but not yet!

"Sorry." Michael was noticeably put down by her stern tone.

He's wet, Paula had told Theresa, but she thought he was nice. She didn't really feel threatened by him. She felt a bit sorry for him, to tell the truth. "Can we meet like this again?" she suggested.

"We can make it a regular date if you like?"

"Don't call it that."

"Don't call it what?"

"Date. It's not a date. Just a meeting." She thought she had better be firm about this. She didn't want him getting ideas above his station, especially when she wasn't even selling platform tickets, yet.

"Yes, of course," he said.

"We can sit together and talk," she said. "I'd like that."

"Me too." It's a start, he thought.

"And can I ask you to stick with me at the disco tonight? To stop any boys from bothering me?"

"Who are you going to get to stop me from bothering you, though?" Michael decided that it was luck-pushing time. He could always claim it was just another joke, he thought. He put his arm around her.

She didn't panic, this time. She just folded her arms, and stared him in the face with a very disapproving look, like it said in her book. She wasn't afraid of them, she told herself. She had one of them at home, and another who had left home. They were both big softies, and she told herself this one was too. He took his arm away. She was right.

When he stood up, she decided to get her revenge. She pushed him hard from behind, so hard that he slipped and fell. "Just try it again," she told him, as he picked himself up, "and I'll floor you properly. I know how."

Michael felt compelled to retaliate to this provocation. "Oh yes! Physical contact, love it!" He pushed her back as she got up. She stumbled, but stayed on her feet.

Growing up with a baby sister had made Michael realise that you were a mug if you bothered with that mustn't-hit-girls rubbish. You were alright so long as you hit them in the right places, he thought: arms, face, back, hair, feet, and nowhere else. That way you could still duff them up good, and they couldn't touch you for it.

Theresa recovered her balance and faced him.

"Evens?" he asked.

She didn't think so, but agreed on a truce.

They walked back across the field together. "I hate the way we're all supposed to want the same things," she said. "You're sixteen, so you have to behave Sixteen: go to discos, dress up, and put so much gunge on your hair and face that it seeps through and dissolves most of your braincells."

"I can't imagine who you might be thinking about there, Treez."

Well, it hadn't been a cuddle, Michael thought, but it was a start.

"Where did you go at Break?"

"Mind your own business." Michael sat by the hi-fi, organising his records and tapes.

"You were with Treez, weren't you?"

"Was I?"

"Yes, you were seen coming out of the English block. Where did you go?"

"Somewhere your gymslip mafia couldn't find us."

"It's not the gymslip mafia; it's the Brownie Pack. What were you and her doing?"

"We were talking."

"Oh yeah? What else?"

"Nothing else."

"I bet."

"I'm sure that you do find it hard to understand what I do, given the enormous gap between the sizes of our IQs."

"What?"

"See what I mean," he said.

"You must have been up to something," Lin reckoned. "She wouldn't say anything either. Reckon you'll make it to the cloakroom with her tonight, do you?"

"Is that what I reckon then Lin?" Michael was getting annoyed. Much more of this and it was Dustbin Time, he thought.

"What you going to wear than?" she enquired.

"I don't know, Lin, what am I going to wear?"

"I think you should wear that jacket mum bought you in the sale."

"If you say so, Sis." He did want her advice, really. He did want to look good on the night.

"What about trousers?" she asked.

"Yes, I shall probably wear some of those."

"Which ones?"

"Clean ones?"

"Don't worry, I'll sort you out later on." Michael thought being "sorted out" by the sister creature was something he was entitled to worry about. "Oh, I just know it's going to be great tonight," she said. "I can't wait, can you?"

"I think I can just about control myself."

"Are you going to dance with me?"

"Not if I can help it."

"Oh why not?"

"Because I'm not going to, that's why not." For Michael the idea of dancing with Lin was on the same sort of level as kissing the cat.

"You don't know how, do you?" she said.

"It's not a question of not knowing how."

"Yes it is!" Lin taunted. "Micky doesn't know how to get down and boogie!"

"Micky doesn't want to get down and boogie!"

"Oh it's easy." Lin switched on the stereo. "Come on, I'll show you." She put on a tape, and started to dance in front of Michael. "Come on Micky," she shouted, pulling Michael to his feet. He stood motionless as she pranced around him. She stopped the music, but only to change the tape.

"I know what," she said. She put on a slow dance number, and before he could escape, ran over and grabbed him in both arms: "Now isn't this nice?" she said as she dragged him slowly across the carpet.

"Delightful," he said, scarcely enthusiastic.

"Well put your arms around me then," she demanded.

Michael lifted his arms from his sides, and placed them on her shoulders. Slowly, he moved them onto her neck, and began to throttle her. He let go when she pinched him hard on his back. "Don't mess about!" she snapped.

"Well let go of me then!"

"Alright." She relaxed her grip on him. She took hold of one of his hands; placed his other hand on her waist, and put her free hand on his shoulder: "We'll do it like this, OK?" Michael accepted this compromise. They swayed together to the music.

"Well Bigbruv, you'll be my number one boy tonight. Don't look like I'll be seeing much of Jimmy."

"What's this Louise like?" Michael asked, deciding to just get on with it, now that she had got hold of him.

83

"Ask any Fifth Year boy, he'll probably know," said Lin, cattily.

"Charming, witty and sophisticated, is she?"

"No, nothing like me."

"Sounds just his type then."

"I was beginning to think he might be changing. For a while I thought he was after one girl for her mind as well as her body."

"Who was that?"

"Oh, just some girl," she said.

Michael stopped reading the titles on the bookshelf, and looked down at the sister creature. She was humming the music softly, and guiding him round gently with her claws retracted, a new experience for him. She noticed he was looking at her, but seemed to ignore him. For the first time ever, he saw her as attractive, in a special sort of way. Michael had seen James hug and kiss both his sisters, including the little one who was only twelve. He had, up till now, considered this behaviour either soppy or sick, but looking now at the sister creature, his sister, he realised for the first time what it was like. It wasn't like that at all. It was really nice. She was an attractive girl, and he felt proud. He kept dancing.

Michael and Lin didn't hear when their mother came in: "Lin, I've told you about playing that so loud . . . Oh . . ." She noticed the two of them still dancing. "Am I in the wrong house?"

"I'm teaching Micky how to dance," said Lin. "He's coming to the disco tonight."

"You mean Michael is actually going out?" June could not quite believe it.

"Yes, and he's got a girlfr . . . Ow!" Lin cried out as Michael stamped on her foot, to stop her speaking the G word. The attractive girl had turned back into the sister creature.

"Well that's lovely," said June. "You'll want your tea early then?"

"Please," said Lin.

"Michael, what are you going to wear, darling?"

"Don't you start as well," Michael warned.

"Oh don't worry Mum, I'll sort him out," said Lin. "I'll have him looking so sexy, they'll all want to dance with him."

"Hold still!"

Lin pushed Michael's head down over the edge of the bath.

"It's going in my eyes!"

For Michael this was the ultimate humiliation. She not only had him on his knees and naked, save for a towel, she was pouring all of her lotions and potions all over his head as well.

"You want to look beautiful, you have to suffer a little." She slapped shampoo onto his head.

"You don't make yourself suffer then, do you?"

"Shut up!" She gave him a smack on the head. He was being a terrible fidget, but really she was enjoying having him in her power like this. "Did you wash yourself properly under the shower?" She talked to him as though he were a little baby, which he was really, she thought.

"No, I stood at the far end of the bath to stop any water getting on me."

"It wouldn't surprise me." She felt his cheek. "You haven't shaved," she complained.

"Oh sorry. You want me to stand under the shower with an electric razor do you? Fine!"

Lin rinsed his hair, after which he stood up and began to dry it. Escape, he thought.

"Hang on. Not finished yet." She took a bottle from the window-ledge.

Michael backed away from her. "I'm not having that gunge!"

"It's conditioner." Lin poured some out. "It's for your split ends."

"I don't care if my ends are split, you are not putting pink snot on my hair." He was out of the door before she could do anything. She rinsed her hand under the tap, and went looking for him.

Sitting on his bed with his old jeans on, Michael thought he had finally escaped Lin's attentions, but it was not to be. "Not finished yet," she repeated. She was standing in the doorway, armed with a hairbrush, and her own special heavy-calibre hair drier. She plugged in, switched on, and jumped onto the bed behind him.

"The Royal Marines used those in the Falklands to shoot down helicopters," he said, as she began her attack.

"What?" She couldn't hear him, and wouldn't have known what he was talking about anyway.

"Ow!" Michael protested as she dragged the brush over his head.

"Well you do it then," she shouted above the noise of the hair-drier, and handed him the brush. He took over, much more delicately. "Not like that!" She objected to his parting.

He snapped back at her. "I thought I was doing it!"

She finished drying his hair, then handed him a mirror. "There you are," she said. "Normally, that would be four pounds fifty, but I'll settle for a thank you now, and a dance later on."

Michael held up the mirror, and cautiously felt the sides of his head. "You have just barbecued my ears," he said.

With Michael conducting a full scale inspection for damage, Lin decided to seize her chance; she ran out to the bathroom and ran back, carrying an anti-perspirant spray. With his arm lifted, he was an easy target: "Got ya," she cried, and managed to strike under the other arm as well before he snatched the spray from her.

"SilkySoft!" Michael read the label with a mixture of disbelief and fear. "Lasting protection with the fragrance of a summer rose garden." He raised his arm to check this claim: "Oh no it isn't," he declared, with relief.

"It's not for you," Lin explained, "it's for any poor girl who gets near you."

"Oh Sis, you say the nicest things sometimes." Michael was finally able to put on his shirt.

"It's alright for you boys, you're taller than us," explained Lin. "If we want to get romantic, look where our faces end up."

"Any boy who got that close to you would pass out from the hair spray fumes." Michael began to tuck his shirt into his jeans.

"No. You are not wearing those."

"They're clean!"

"They're too scruffy. You'll stand out a mile." She began to search through his wardrobe for something acceptable.

"I'm beginning to sympathise with all those dolls you used to pull the arms and legs off," he said.

"I never did that. That was you and your stupid Action Man, torturing them."

"Interrogating them. They were terrorists."

"There you are . . ." She threw a pair of trousers onto the bed, "put those on." He picked up the trousers, and stood waiting, looking at her. For a moment, she wondered why he had turned statue, then realised: "Oh come on," she said, "you're not shy are you?"

"Turn around, you," he ordered.

"You saw me topless on holiday, and I didn't mind."

"That is because you are a flasher and a pervert." Michael had minded, especially when any males came past them on the beach, and he had felt it necessary to put towels over both his mother and his sister; exhibitionists the pair of them.

"Sorry." She turned her back and tried not to laugh.

When she was given permission, Lin turned around. "Oh yes," she eyed him up, "that's better." She stood on the bed again to give his hair a final quick brush, straightened his collar at the back, jumped down, and stood back to admire her work. "Cor," she said, "you're not bad, are you?"

"Of course I'm not bad." He wanted to tell her that he thought she looked nice too, but didn't want to risk the reaction that might provoke.

"She'll think so too," said Lin. "Right. Now get rid of that fluff on your face and you'll be irresistible." She picked up her equipment, and headed for the door.

"Thanks Sis," he said, half under his breath.

"S'alright," said Lin. "Don't forget about my dance."

"We're off Mum, OK?" Lin shouted from the hall.

"Wait a minute," June rushed out of the living room.

"Why? What's up?" Lin asked.

"Nothing," June said. "I just wanted to have a look at you both." Lin held onto Michael's arm. "My two babies," said June. "My two lovely children, off out on their first mad teenage rave-up together."

Michael felt embarrassed. "It's only a school disco Mum; all lemonade and the same old people."

"There'll be one new face there. Yours," said June. "Why's that darling? Anyone in particular you're hoping to see?"

"Well, there's this one girl who's been begging me to dance with her," he reported.

"Oh, well she's very welcome to come back here for coffee tonight."

"That's nice to know," said Lin.

June saw them off and tried to think when was the last time they had gone somewhere together. The most recent example she could recall was her firm's Christmas children's party, some five years earlier. That time Lin had been sick after eating too many cakes, while Michael had left ten minutes after she had dropped them both off, and come home on the bus.

"There's normally a shortage of boys at these dos, so we have to grab hold of any we find and not let 'em go," said Lin. "Reckon you could handle that?"

"One way to find out," said Michael.

"I wonder why that is? A load of girls, all dressed up and dying to get their hands on any decent male bod, and they don't come. And quite a few of those that do come only want to sit with their mates and take the piss."

"If you don't take the piss, you have it taken out of you."

"That's stupid," Lin said, "boys are stupid."

"Must be to fancy girls," said Michael.

"Speaking of fancying girls, Micky."

This was what he was going to have to put up with all evening, he thought. "Look, I realise you would find this very difficult to understand, but it is not a question

89

of fancying anyone. Treez is a very nice person, a good friend . . ."

"And you fancy her rotten."

"No," said Michael, "I fancy little Clare Hunter."

"All the boys fancy Clare."

"Yes, and doesn't she know it," he said. "But just because I like someone, it does not follow automatically that I fancy them. Your trouble is you've got 'fancy' on the brain. I agree with Treez, it's the pink snot that does it."

"You fancy Treez, and she fancies you, and you're both too scared to admit it." That was Lin's theory. "I shall tell Clare what you said."

"Tell Clare she can chain me to the bed anytime."

"She's on the door, taking tickets with Jill. You can tell her yourself." Lin knew he wouldn't dare.

"Hi, Lin," said Clare, taking their tickets. "Ready to boogie?"

"I will be."

"Evening Clare. Hiya JB."

"I've brought the brother along," Lin explained.

"So I see." Clare acknowledged Michael's presence, but didn't sound very impressed.

"Hold your hand out, Micky." Jill marked the back of Michael's hand with a large red letter "O".

"What's this Jill; your latest English essay?"

"No Micky, it's your 'A' Level result."

"Has Jimmy arrived yet?" Lin asked.

"He's out on the floor," Clare told her, "finding his way around Louise."

"And how about Treez?" asked Lin. "Has Polly brought her yet?"

"Never mind about Treez," said Clare. "Pol's supposed to be bringing our headache medicine."

"I'm only giving her another half hour," said Jill. "I'm going down the chemist's to get my own after that."

Michael and Lin went inside.

"Alright then Jimbo?" Michael edged his way across to where James was performing his mating display.

"Hello, stranger, welcome to the fun." James turned away from his quest. She was a big girl, Michael managed to notice, but this wasn't very difficult since quite a lot of her was on display.

"Get me a drink Jimmy," she moaned. She had a voice like an air-raid siren, Michael thought.

"In a minute Angel," James said. "Let me talk to my mate first."

"Coke with ice and lemon, I want," she told him. Out of her gaze, James let Michael see him sigh wearily.

"Listen Mike, I can't spend much time chatting, she's getting ever so stroppy."

"I can't imagine what you see in her," Michael lied.

"She's got one or two charming features." James wasn't making any excuses.

"Jimmy. I want a drink." She was getting louder and whinier. The Heinkels must be overhead by now, Michael thought.

"I'll see you, OK." James was led off to the bar.

Lin returned from the bar with two fizzy drinks. "I've just passed Jimmy on the steps, and he didn't even look at me!" She sounded hurt.

"Nice girl, isn't she, I don't think."

"He'll have his hands full with her tonight."

"With any luck, yes."

"A bird in the hand's not worth one in the bushes." Lin placed her drink on a table by the wall. "Come on, dance with me," she said.

Michael looked at her very doubtfully. He didn't mind dancing in the living room, where no one could see, but he didn't want to make a fool of himself in public.

"Well you can't just stand around up here," Lin said. "Either join in, or go and sit in a corner on your own." She started to move.

Michael looked down at her feet, and began to copy her steps. He was awkward, a bit jerky to start with, but he soon relaxed. Lin stopped him a couple of times, to show him some slowed-down moves, which he managed to pick up quite well. He even managed to smile. The song finished and they both went to grab their drinks. "See," said Lin. "Doesn't hurt, does it?"

Michael peered out over the scene. A group of Upper Sixth girls, acquaintances of his, were organised into a circle. They seemed almost unrecognisable in loud and outrageous outfits, instead of their usual drab school plumage. Lin suddenly walked away. He stopped staring at his classmates and looked to see where she had gone.

There was a chorus of screams as the Brownie Girls all greeted each other in turn. They were holding each other's arms, and jumping up and down. Theresa only smiled. Lin waved to Michael, indicating that he should come over.

"Hi Micky," said Zahira. Michael pulled a silly face and made her laugh. Nice kid, Z-Cars, he thought. Shame she'd fallen in with such bad company.

"So, are we boogieing or what?" Jill asked impatiently.

"Well I'm game," said Clare, "but where are all the hunky boys?"

"They'll appear," Paula predicted, "the guys come running when they see I'm around."

"I shall not bother to respond to this provocation," said Michael.

"Micky can boogie, you all wait and see," Lin told them. "You dancing, Zed?" she asked.

"Yeah! Get down!" Zahira's voice was as loud as her crazy trousers.

"And how about you, Treez?" asked Lin.

Theresa looked awkward: "I'd rather give it a miss for now Lin. Sorry."

"Well find a nice corner for us to sit later on," Lin ordered, "and Micky will get you a drink." She gave Michael a firm push in the back, making him step one pace forward towards Theresa.

"Hello Micky."

"Good Evening, and have you been taking the headache medicine as well?"

"What? Oh, no."

"No, neither have I." Michael held up his paper cup. "I'm on this stuff. It rots your teeth instead of your liver. Would you like some?"

"Yes thanks, but I don't want any of that sexist being-bought-drinks-lark. I can buy my own."

"Be my guest. Buy mine as well."

"I will."

My kind of girl, Michael thought.

"You been here long?" Theresa asked, as they went to get drinks.

"No, not long." They collected their drinks, and sat down in an empty corner.

"You been to one of these before?"

"Not Sixth Form. How about you?"

"Nah."

That was it. They had both run out of small talk. It went quiet after that.

Theresa looked around at the scene. Over by the bar some boys were larking about, pushing each other. One of them got most of a drink spilt over him, the rest found this enormously funny. "They're pathetic, aren't they?" she said.

"I think they should be better catered for," said Michael. "It's not a disco they want, is it? It's a playpen."

"Do you think they've been on the medicine?"

"I think everyone has, except me and you. Ah, there's Jimmy. Don't know where his 'Angel' has got to. Perhaps she flapped her wings and flew away to bomb Dresden or something."

James approached them. "Good Evening wallflowers. Who's whispering sweet nothings into whose ear then?"

"Well no one is at the moment, Jim, but you can come and sit on my knee if you like."

"Very kind of you to offer, Mike, but I'm afraid you're too late."

"But where is the lovely Louise?" Michael asked.

"In the cloakroom, waiting for me," James reported. "Can I expect you two to be joining us later on then?"

"We might," said Michael. "We'll come and watch you."

"The McGarvey Masterclass, I like it. I might start selling tickets."

"It'd be the funniest show in town. But if she's out there, why are you in here?"

"Because she wants another drink." James mocked her tone of voice.

"Oh, you're not still into that drinks act, are you?" Michael asked.

"If that's what they want, yes," James said.

"What if they want to be treated as an equal?" Theresa asked.

"Whatever makes them happy," said James.

"Whatever gets your hand up, you mean," Michael suggested.

"Like I say, whatever makes them happy."

Michael stood up and shook James's hand: "Well, good luck old man. We'll send in a search party if you're gone too long, and don't forget to tie yourself with string to the rail, in case you get lost in there."

James moved close to Michael and spoke softly so that Theresa could not hear. Moving off to get the drink, James seemed a little put out by Michael's reply.

"What did he say?"

"He said I should be careful because I was going where no man had gone before."

"I see."

"And so I told him where he got off."

"Follow that." Theresa thought out loud, quite shocked.

"Don't make too much of it," said Michael. "Jim's my mate, I'm always telling him that, and worse."

"How come you're both so nasty to each other? I thought we were the ones who were supposed to be bitchy?"

"You are," said Michael. "This is the opposite."

"I don't see the difference."

"Bitchy is when you pretend you like someone, most of the time, but occasionally let it slip that you don't. Boys don't do that; if they don't like someone, they just ignore them. But when you're mates with someone, you take the piss all the time."

"Seems a strange way of being 'mates' to me."

"It's a kind of test," Michael tried to explain: "You

95

insult someone, you're daring them to take offence."

"Testing the relationship?" Theresa was beginning to understand.

"Yeah, that's right. That way you know who your mates are."

"Girls just ask."

"Well they would, wouldn't they?" Michael sneered. "But a boy can't look his mate in the eye and say 'hey pal, I think you're great.' He might get the wrong idea."

"Why should he? Girls don't get the wrong idea."

"But girls are girls," said Michael. "They can hold hands and hug each other; and they're allowed to cry."

"You think it's easier being a woman than a man, do you?"

"Who mentioned men and women? Not me. No. It's a man's world, and that's the problem; you've got to 'Be a Man'. Well, you haven't got to but we're supposed to; us fellahs."

"It's other men that say that, though, and other boys."

"It's your lot too."

"How's that?"

"Those ferret-pack girls Sis hangs out with," said Michael. "They keep going on about 'hunky bods' and 'guys'. Guys! Those are for tents!"

"They think you're wet."

"Yes, and I think they're potty. I mean I go for Clare Hunter, but she's never going to play Doctors and Nurses with me, not while she can attract the gorillas."

"I'm not like that."

"I know," said Michael. "Do you fancy a game of Doctors and Nurses?"

"Mum's got all the equipment at home. I'll give you a vasectomy if you like?"

That one shut him up.

"I hope we're not interrupting anything." Lin led the girls into Michael and Theresa's corner.

"No," said Michael, "Treez was just threatening to mutilate me, that's all."

"I didn't know you were into S and M, Treez," said Clare.

"I don't even know what it is."

"Sado-masochism," Paula explained.

"Flagellation and that," Lin added.

"Buggery," Clare recited, "is a pain in the arse!"

"Incest is relatively boring . . ." Paula joined in with the routine.

Jill delivered the punchline: "But you can't beat flagellation!"

"No," added Clare, "but you can beat a masochist!"

The girls giggled, convulsed and screamed.

"Well we were having an intelligent conversation," said Theresa.

"You'll have to excuse us . . ." Lin gasped for breath. ". . . but I think we've all had a bit too much fizzy orange."

"Don't tell Mrs Garrett," said Zahira, in between the collective fits of laughter. Slowly, the spasms subsided.

"Where is Jimmy?" Lin asked.

"In the cloakroom," said Michael.

"Whoooa!" A chorus went up.

"And where," Lin asked, "as if I didn't know, is Louise?"

"I'll give you three guesses," said Michael.

"Right," said Lin, "is she on the dance floor?"

"Noooo," said the chorus.

"Is she . . . in the bog, then?"

"Noooo!"

"Thennn," said Lin, "she must be . . ."

Zahira beat Lin to it: "Snogging with Jimmy!"

Jill Bryce began a rendition of the Snog Song, which

had its origins in the Monty Python Spam Song, but had a new, and equally subtle lyric: "Snog, snog, snog, snog. Snog, snog, snog, snog . . ." went the girls.

Lin stood up, and waved to stop the singing. "We have got a problem." She moved behind Michael, and placed her hands on his shoulders. "We have only got one boy," she said, "my brother and you can't all snog him at once."

"Yes we can!" Jill insisted. The Snog Song began to re-assert itself, but Lin quickly cut it short.

"No," said Lin, "you shouldn't." She patted him on the head. "He's spoken for tonight," she said. "Wish I was."

"Get stuck in there, Treez," said Clare.

"Make sure he blows on his hands first though," Jill advised.

Theresa felt very uncomfortable with the way they were all looking at her, as though they were all expecting her to disappear off to the cloakroom with Michael at any moment.

"I have an announcement to make." Lin suddenly raised a finger. "I've got to go to the loo."

"I'm coming with you," said Paula.

"So am I," said Clare.

"Me too," said Jill.

"Yeah," said Zahira. They all skipped off in a great, giggling mass.

Michael and Theresa looked at each other, both slightly dazed.

"Nice girls," said Michael. "Aren't they?"

"Yes," Theresa agreed in the same sort of tone, "but I don't think I want to be here when they come back, not while they're in that mood."

"Well if we disappeared, they're going to come to certain conclusions."

Nearby, a girl sitting on her own was trying to ignore the attentions of three boys, who were obviously bothering her. Theresa did not want to be left alone by Michael. "What can we do?" she asked him.

"Well I know what I'd like to do," Michael said.

"What's that?" Theresa asked, a little suspicious.

"I'd like to ask you," he said, terribly formally, "if you'd dance with me?"

"I can't dance."

"Prove it." He stood up. "Please." He held out his hand.

"Promise me you won't laugh?"

"No. You look daft and I'll laugh. You want phony compliments, go see Jim in the cloakroom."

She got to her feet, without taking his hand, and followed him over to the floor, not knowing what on earth she was supposed to do. On the way down the steps, he grabbed her hand anyway, and guided her out to a space.

"Just relax and do whatever you feel like," Michael shouted into her ear, as if he knew what he was talking about. He began to reproduce some of Lin's steps. Theresa shuffled about, very self-consciously.

Michael looked around him at the other dancers. Among the congregation, he spotted something that looked familiar, it appeared now and again, popping in and out of view; it was Roland's head. Michael too was spotted, and soon a small bouncing creature came to Michael and Theresa's side.

"This is good this, innit?" said Roland.

"It's meant to be a bop, not a hop," Michael told him.

"You should try it . . ." Roland carried on bouncing, "it don't half get the girls going."

"No it doesn't Sonny," said Michael. "It might possibly

arouse some interest from a sex-starved kangeroo, but that's all."

"Well watch this then. Hi Treez!" He bounded from one side of her to the other, pushing down on her shoulders to boost himself.

"No Sonny, stop it!" she said, laughing, trying to fight him off.

"Sonny!"

Above all the noise, Lin's voice screeched out across the floor, followed by a series of calls from the other girls. Roland broke away, leapt over, and landed half way up Lin, with her lifting him up by the waist. She dropped him to the ground, and they all rushed over to what had been Michael and Theresa's own little space. They formed a circle, taking in Michael and Theresa without giving them any chance to decline.

"Get down, Micky," someone shouted, so Michael sat on the floor. He was pulled to his feet, and the serious dancing began. Everyone was swept up together by the mood: Lin and Paula strutted emphatically, Clare slunk about, watched by Michael and half a dozen other boys within range of her. Theresa still shuffled her feet, but also waved her arms quite elegantly. Jill waved her arms as well, and several times caught people in the face with them. Michael began to develop some original steps, most of them resulting from his attempts to stay dancing next to Theresa but opposite Clare. Zahira tried to copy what everyone else did. And Roland bounced. They danced for well over an hour without stopping, but nobody cared about the time.

With only half an hour remaining, the first of the slow dances began. In no time the floor became crowded, as quite a few boys who had spent all evening seated, went out in search of girls. Lin and Paula quickly grabbed themselves partners. Clare Hunter was asked three times in quick succession, each one refused. One of her rejects looked for a substitute, and his attention fell upon Theresa. No thank you, she said, but he was persistent. But for this intrusion, Michael would probably not have had the guts to ask her. "Sorry," he said, "she's with me." Michael took hold of Theresa to emphasise the point, and the unwelcome suitor backed off.

"Thanks." Theresa at first expected Michael to leave it at that, but he kept hold of her, in the manner Lin had shown him, and they moved gently together in time with the music.

Theresa felt nervous. Afraid he might move his hand. Afraid she might trip over her own feet. She looked at her feet, most of the time. When she looked up, Michael quickly stopped staring at her. All of Michael's attentions were focussed on the palm of his right hand. He could feel the clear curve in and out of her waist. One word held onto his mind: girl.

When the song finished, he dropped her hand and thanked her. She smiled at him. Another slow song began, and there was considerable movement on the floor, as boys and girls searched for new partners in an adolescent version of musical chairs. Afraid that she might be bothered again by someone, Theresa took hold of Michael once more, not clinging for protection, but as a visible discouragement to any boy who rated his chances. What Theresa hadn't allowed for though, was that she wasn't the only one in demand.

"Put him down, Treez, you've had your go. My turn now." Lin took Michael for the dance. Theresa, left standing on her own, could only drift off into the corner.

Michael had been quite encouraged by Theresa seeming to want a second dance, and continued to keep an eye on her whilst dancing with Lin.

"Enjoying yourself then?" Lin asked.

"I was till you showed up."

"She's not going anywhere. She's only got eyes for you. I've been watching."

"So why did you break us up then? I was going to demonstrate that other way of dancing together you showed me."

"You mustn't. That would have been pushing your luck."

"It's my luck, I'll push it if I want."

"You don't have two dances in a row with the same person," Lin explained, "not unless you want to get very seriously friendly, and you were the one who said you didn't fancy her. Remember?"

"She wanted to carry on."

"Makes no difference. You don't know the rules yet, and neither does she."

"Maybe we want to make our own rules?"

"The rules are the same for everyone," said Lin. "You have to stick to the rules, or you end up crying."

"OK, Smartarse, so how do I get to learn these magic rules then?"

"You stick with me, Bigbruv," she said, digging him in the stomach. She closed her eyes, and tried to imagine that he was someone else, the person she'd most rather be dancing with tonight.

"Treez."

Standing in the corner, trying not to draw attention to herself, Theresa was startled to hear her name. She turned around to see who was calling. "Jimmy?" she said.

"Have you seen Lin anywhere?"

"She's out there, with Micky. Do you want me to get her?"

"No." James spotted them. "Mustn't intrude on their happy families act."

"Is there something wrong?"

"You could say that."

"Well, what is it?" Theresa asked.

"Oh, you're a good sort. I reckon you'd understand. Please will you come somewhere quiet so I can explain?" Theresa looked at him suspiciously. "I swear I'm not up to any tricks," he said.

"Where?" Theresa was very doubtful about this indeed.

"Ah, well the only quiet place is the cloakroom," said James, "but I promise I'm not trying it on, honest." Theresa looked at him angrily. "Or there's the car park. Do you fancy the car park?"

"I'm telling you Jimmy," said Theresa, stepping around a couple of cloakroom canoodlers, "I've got a book on self-defence for women; you try anything, and I shall scream right into your face."

"I won't." James sat down and stared at the wall.

Theresa gazed down at him. He looked rough. "Did you and her have a fight or something?"

"Not a fight, no. I just told her to piss off, that's all."

"Why?" Theresa did not sit down, but leaned against the hanger rails a few feet away from him.

"Because all the time it was get me this, get me that, and I'm not some flaming dog-on-a-lead."

"I thought we were supposed to be the dogs?"

"What? Oh yeah, I know. I've said that, I admit. You

103

see a mate with some ugly girl, what's this, you say, One Man And His Dog?"

"Do you have any idea how insulting that sounds?"

"Listen Treez, some girls are dogs. I know; no manners, no morals, no value."

"What does that make you for chasing after them, then?"

"That's a point," said James. "If you want that, you must be that yourself." James's head sank into his hands. "I've paid three times to get in here tonight," he said. "God, I feel so rotten, I reckon I might even go to confession tomorrow and tell the truth for once!"

"So what am I? A surrogate priest?"

"Father Ray doesn't understand," said James. "He is a celibate old twit."

"I'm a celibate young agnostic."

"You're nicer looking than him, though."

Lin had come out to look for Theresa, and spotted her head among the hanger rails. "Treez, what are you doing out here?"

"She's letting me cry on her shoulder," James called. Lin came to where Theresa was standing, and saw him. "I came looking for you," he said.

"It's that Louise, isn't it?" She sat beside him, and patted him on both knees. "Tell me all about it."

James held out his arms to Lin, and she advanced herself into them. James looked across at Theresa, standing and watching it all: "Different class, this one," he said. James and Lin stroked each other's backs. "Well, thanks for listening Treez," said James. "Bye bye now."

"Oh, sorry," she said, and hastily made an exit.

"What are you doing now?" Michael asked, as Roland

went around all the tables, picking up any unclaimed paper cups.

"I'm parched." Roland poured a few drops from one cup into another. He repeated this process several times. "I've nearly got a mouthful here," he said.

"Have you considered the purchase of a full cupful?"

"That's alright Micky, you don't have to buy me one." Roland swallowed his orange/lemon and lime/ginger beer/cola cocktail. "Nice," he said.

Theresa joined the two boys.

"Where did you get to?" Michael asked.

In the cloakroom with Jimmy McGarvey? No, she thought: "To the loo," she said.

"Where's Lin?" Michael asked.

"In the cloakroom with Jimmy McGarvey," she said.

Michael looked at his watch: "Well, I'll give them five minutes, before I go and accidentally discover them."

"Alright children, put everything down, do everything up. It's nearly time for the bell to go."

Michael was right. Quite a few people had come out to the cloakroom, getting ready to leave, so James and Lin were sitting side by side, not touching. James stood up. "I suppose I'd better be going."

"Alright then," said Lin, also rising. "I'll see you tomorrow night."

"I'll give you a call." James kissed her on the cheek, then turned to Michael: "Well Mike, from what Lin says, it sounds like you've had a better evening than me. This time."

"You're the one that's had two in the cloakroom," Michael told him.

"You've got a lot to learn mate," said James, "and

so have I. See you." He slapped Michael on the back.

In all corners of the cloakroom, Michael could see people saying goodbye; some kissing, some holding hands, some not.

"So what do you think of stupid old school discos now then?" Lin asked.

"Well I expect they must be really boring when I don't turn up," said Michael.

"This is one of the best bits," said Lin. "At the end, you get to kiss all your best friends."

"Is it a private game, or can anyone join in?" Roland appeared next to Michael.

"I'm not kissing him," said Michael.

"Oh, why not?" said Roland.

"I am," said Lin, and did so.

Roland slapped his own face on the spot where she had made contact, slowly pulling his hand away as if clutching something small and precious. "I shall keep that," he said, putting it in his pocket.

Someone called Lin's name, and she went to where the girls were standing, and joined in a round of hugs. Roland also joined them, and got hugged by them all, including Clare Hunter. Jammy little sod, Michael thought. Then Michael noticed Theresa.

"Are you going straight off home?" He was hoping she might come back for coffee.

"I'd better," she said. "I don't want to have to use late buses on a Friday night."

"Oh, yeah," he said.

"It's been good, hasn't it?"

"Yeah."

"Well, I'll see you in school on Monday, shall I?"

"Yeah."

"We'll go to our meeting place at break?"

"Yeah," he said. It was all he could get himself to say.

"Bye then." She couldn't think of anything else to say.

"Yeah," he said, and she went.

"So did you kiss her?" Lin asked, as she walked out of the school with Michael. He said nothing. "Never mind," she said. "You will next time."

"What next time?" He was sick with himself for letting her go like she had.

"Up to you," Lin said. "You could ask her out."

"She's not an alcoholic like you, you know."

"There's lots of places apart from pubs," said Lin. "Take her to the pictures. She likes foreign films that you can't understand. But don't go in the back row, that's only for when you're both planning to have a snog, it's . . ."

"In the rules," Michael finished the sentence for her.

"You're learning, Bigbruv," she said, taking his arm.

Chapter 4

"Thanks Jimmy," said Lin, as James handed her a glass, and sat down next to her in a quiet corner of the Argie Pub.

"Make the most of it," he said. "If you want another one, you'll have to get it yourself." Come out for a drink, he had said, and a drink he had meant. James was broke.

"I am perfectly capable of buying my own drinks, Jimmy!"

"You're pretty good at getting other people to buy them for you n'all. Mike's right; girls should pay for their share."

"That sounds like Treez talking to me," said Lin. "She's into all that feminist stuff." Lin struggled to remember what Theresa had said the other day: "What was it? Oh yeah: being taken out by a man is a form of prostitution. The service varies, the payment varies, but the woman is always exploited," she recited.

"It's the daft ones that get exploited," said James, "male and female."

"Oh how can it be exploiting someone to treat them? Suppose you took me somewhere for a meal one evening, for example?"

"Bag of chips, you mean?"

"Nowhere expensive; let's say that Italian place down by the station, for example, and suppose I had the veal in cream sauce, shall we say, with the special mushrooms and selection of vegetables . . ."

"Not that you're actually suggesting . . ."

"No, just supposing," said Lin. "Next Saturday, for example. We'll say the veal, and afterwards the ice cream, and some of that stuff I like to drink, what's it called?"

"The EEC wine lake?"

"No, it's sparkling white wine; Lambroghini, I think it's called. We'll have plenty of that. We could sit and talk by candlelight. Walk home, holding hands in the moonlight. Then you could come in for coffee. And after that, we could have one of our cuddles. Oh what a lovely idea!" No, not really, thought James. "Now you can't tell me that's exploitation," said Lin.

"Well what is it then?"

"Romance."

"What? Me spending all my money on you? Sounds more like tragedy to me."

This was the big night, and Lin was not going to be put off: "Alright then, I'll pay," she said.

"You?" James was staggered.

"Me. I owe it to you, all the times you've treated me."

"This is true."

"So long as what you said last night was the truth." Lin came to the point. "About me being the best and all that."

"Did I say that?" James teased her.

"You know you did. And you said your love 'em and leave 'em days were over."

"What I said," James recounted, "was that in future, I wasn't going to be any girl's dog-on-a-lead; not for any reason."

"Oh, I wouldn't do that to you, Jimmy."

"You'd have me chained, muzzled, and off to the vet's probably, if you got the chance."

"I really want to go out with you Jimmy, and I don't want no one else."

"Don't want *no one* else? No wonder you're re-taking your English."

"Jimmy! I'm being serious here. I want you and me to go together."

"Go?" James spat the word out. "You know what that means?"

"Of course I know, that's why I'm asking."

"It means eng'ged to be eng'ged," said James, distastefully. "Much more of this and you'll be starting to think about the E word."

"What? Engaged?"

"Don't mention the E word!"

"I don't want to marry you!" cried Lin, astonished, mentioning the M word; an even greater obscenity. James looked around anxiously, in case there was anybody in tonight who knew him and might think he was proposing, or something. "Marriage is stupid," said Lin.

"Well, so are you," James said. "You're a soppy, possessive little dipsomaniac who always has to have everything her own way. A dog-on-a-lead is what you're after, alright; preferably a St Bernard with a full barrel of brandy."

"I hate you!" Lin went into a sulk.

James attempted to bring her out of it. "Hey, I was only messing you about. I said you were my best girl, and I meant it."

She continued to stare into the ashtray.

"You wait till I pass my driving test," he said, nudging her. "You can be my first passenger. I'll take you up town if you like, or out into the country."

"What about the seaside?" Lin murmured.

"It's a bit far to the coast, but we could go to the watersports centre?"

"What about the seaside?" she repeated, sternly.

He got the message. "Alright, the seaside," he said, and her head lifted. "Wherever you want," he said.

"France," she demanded. "Disneyland." Geography was one of several exams Lin had managed to fail the previous summer.

"In this country," he corrected himself, "so long as we can get there and back in a day. But don't you go buying me a Jimmy and Lin sun-visor, because if you do, then I'll take you, and it, to the seaside, and leave you there with it. OK?"

"I love you, Jimmy," she said.

"I wish you'd make your mind up."

"Hi Micky," said Lin, "what's the news?"

Michael did not look up from the Sunday paper. "Arms control experts expect the Superpower talks in Geneva to collapse," he said. "Growing Third World debts mean that the international economy may be on the brink of collapse and England's batting has already collapsed, under the onslaught of the vicious Sri Lankan medium-pacers."

"Is that all?" said Lin, unmoved. Michael would have liked to have been allowed to find out what the news was in peace, but Lin was not going to leave him alone until she had announced her big story: "Nothing about me?" she asked.

"I don't know, I'll have a look." Michael turned the pages. "Yes, there's something here." He noticed an article: "The earth's ozone layer is being destroyed; cosmic radiation is going to penetrate the atmosphere, and we're all going to die. Scientists say that this is mainly due to the extensive use of aerosols in Western countries. Satellite observation indicates that most of the pollution is hairspray, coming from Lin's bedroom."

"It doesn't say that!" She looked over his shoulder. "Come on," she said, "ask me my news."

"No." Michael continued to study the paper.

"Ask me!" Lin insisted and began to pinch Michael's back.

"What's your news, Lin?" Michael decided that this was the only way he was going to get rid of her.

"Jimmy and me are going together," she announced, proudly.

"Well hurry up and go then, the pair of you."

"No, stupid, not going; *going*!"

"Gone!" said Michael.

"It means he's my boyfriend, and I'm his girlfriend," she explained. "When he's passed his test, he's going to take me for a ride in his car."

Michael sniggered. "McGarvey in a motor." He considered this prospect. "I bet he'll have a special refrigerated rear window fitted to make the glass steam up at the touch of a button."

"Well that's where you're wrong, Clever Dick, because he's turned over a new leaf. He told me at the disco."

"And you believed him, did you?"

"Yes I did, and so would you if you'd heard him. He's going to teach me how to drive. I can't actually drive the car yet, so we'll have to practise first of all on the sofa."

Michael shook his head and tried not to laugh.

Lin sat down and picked up a cushion for a steering wheel. "The first thing I've got to learn is where the pedals are."

"What I want to know," said Michael, between sniggers, "is how is he going to demonstrate the use of the handbrake?"

Lin threw the cushion and hit Michael right in the face. "He's changed, I know he has," she said, "and I thought

112

you had too. I thought you might have stopped being such a big kid now that you've finally started courting."

"You what?"

"You and Treez."

"I am not courting Treez!"

"Yes you are. You stuck to her all night at the disco, like a great big zit!"

"I'm surprised you can remember Friday night. You were so pissed."

"I remember you wanted to kiss her, but you didn't have the bottle, did you?"

"You were the one on the bottle, as usual!"

"Alright then. Where will you be at break tomorrow in school? I bet you'll be wherever it is you go with her, just like you were all last week."

"Haven't found out where it is then yet?"

Lin-baiting was a game Michael was more than good at. He always managed to make her blow her top: "No!" she squealed, "that's because I haven't been looking! Because I wanted to leave you and her in peace! So that you could become friends. And I thought: with you and her friends, and me and Jimmy friends, and me and her friends, and you and him friends, I thought we could all be friends," Lin recounted, breathlessly, "and we could all be so happy!" She finished with a scream, then ran out of the room and up the stairs. Michael took a long breath, threw down the paper, and went to find her.

Lin was lying face down on the bed when Michael came into her room. When she noticed him, she pulled the pillow over her head.

"Come on, Sis."

"Piss off," came the muffled shout from under the

pillow. He never knew when she would go like this. He knew he had to get her out of it, now.

"Oh! You said a naughty word," Michael chanted, "I'm telling Mum." He sat at the foot of the bed. "I'm very sorry Lin, please come out."

She kicked him off the bed.

"Alright, if that's the way you want to play it," he said. "I haven't done this to you for years, and I know it's a bit drastic, but you leave me no alternative."

Michael stood on a stool, and opened the large cupboard above the dressing-table. Digging into an old cardboard box, he found what he was looking for. "This is the one," he said. "This is the one you used to like." He sat on the floor beside the bed, and began to read: "Once upon a time," Michael read, "there were three bears, a mummy bear, a daddy bear, and a little baby bear . . ."

Michael read the story, using different silly voices for each character, just like he had used to do: "So Goldi-locks tried the first bowl of porridge, oooh, she said, that's too hot!" After a few lines, Lin came out from under the pillow. She sat up, folded her arms, and stared stonily at him. "Then she tried the second bowl, oooh, she said, that's too cold! And so Goldilocks tried the third bowl . . . Come on, you miserable cow; laugh!" Michael reached out and began to tickle Lin under the arm.

The book went flying.

"And after that," said Michael, "we had a pillow-fight."

"Aren't you both rather old to be behaving like that?" Theresa asked Michael, sitting alongside him on their bench.

"It was funny," said Michael. "It was just like we were

kids again; except that when we used to have pillow fights it was much more violent."

"Alan and Gordon never used to like me joining in with anything they were doing."

"Those are your brothers?"

"Yes. Alan's the oldest. He's off and married, and Gordon's away too now, in his final year."

"What? Prison?"

"University," said Theresa, "it's much the same, except that the food's worse, or so he says."

"You're the baby of the family then?"

"Yes. Well, not any more, there's a new one of those. I'm the auntie of the family now."

"Auntie Treez?"

"I'm only Treez at school; at home I'm Ter-ai-ser," said Theresa, grandly.

"Which do you prefer?"

"Neither, really," she said. "I think I'd rather be French; zen ah could be Thérèse."

"You wouldn't half stand out, with that Norwegian accent."

"I don't think my parents realised that they were giving me a joke-name. Trees-are-green; try surviving with that in a junior school playground. How about you, Micky-Michael-Mike; which do you prefer?"

"Sir."

"Well I'm sorry, but to me you were always Micky, the famous big brother, the one Lin never used to stop going on about."

"I never knew this."

"Oh yes," she said, "it was always Micky did this, Micky did that, Micky let me borrow this."

"I never let her borrow anything. She steals the lot! All my records, my radio-cassettes; everything."

"She was mad about you. I could never understand why, because you were always so rotten to her."

"She was a thieving little pest who wouldn't leave me alone. She used to drive me up the wall."

"She loves you."

"I know," Michael conceded.

"And do you love her too?"

"Yes," said Michael, a little bashfully. "Only don't tell her I said that, will you?"

"I don't see why people shouldn't be able to let each other know how much they like each other. What's wrong with that?" Theresa asked.

She was enjoying this getting-to-know-you exercise, and had decided that she was going to do something she was curious about, if he kept being serious and didn't make any cheap remarks.

"Well, nothing, I suppose," said Michael.

"That's nice," said Theresa. "I think you're very nice." It was time, she decided.

Tentatively, Theresa leaned forward towards Michael, and planted a kiss on his cheek. Michael gave out a muted yelp. "That's what I think of you," she said, drawing back.

"That's nice to know." He was stunned into complete immobility.

"I'm glad you understand," she said. "I was afraid you might think I was leading you on. You don't think that, do you?"

"No, of course not," he said, recovering. "Feel free to do that again, whenever you like. I shan't hold it against you, in any way."

"It wasn't meant to be the start of a regular course of treatment," she said. "It was just a one-off. Just to let you know."

"Thanks very much." Michael was still a little catatonic.

What it was, in fact, was that she had decided that it was about time she kissed one, and this one looked as good as any.

"You can do the same to me . . ." she raised her head slightly, ". . . if you want to." She thought it best to do it properly, both ends up.

At first, he was stunned, but overcoming his paralysis, Michael craned out his neck, and made contact with his lips. It was a bad shot, more on the chin than on the cheek, but before he could correct this she had placed herself just out of range, not allowing him to give any more than he had got.

"Congratulations." She shook his hand. "You're the first non-relative male who's ever done that."

"Do I get a certificate?"

"I'll think about it," she said. "Meantime, there's a really good new film on in town. Do you want to go and see it?"

What film, he thought? Bugger the film, he thought. "Yeah. Love to," he said.

"Good," she said. "We can go together. How about tomorrow night?"

"Fine."

Yes fine, he thought. Yippee! Fan-bloody-tastic!

"And do you think Sonny would like to come too?" she asked him. "It'd be good for us to get together as a threesome, don't you think?"

"Yeah. Wonderful."

Cow, he thought. Cow. Cow! Cow!!

"Lin," said Michael, "you busy?"

"No, why?" She put down her magazine and looked up at him.

117

"Can you stand up, please?"

"What for?" She did as he requested, not having any idea why. "Hey!" She noticed that he was armed. "That's my eyebrow pencil," she cried.

"Listen, just stay still for a while, and I'll let you borrow my new headphones, anytime you want, OK."

"Alright." She turned her head to try to follow him. "What you going to do?"

"I am conducting a scientific experiment," he said, wrenching her head back into a forward-facing position. "Now I need an attractive girl for this, but I suppose you'll do. Now stay completely still."

She held her head still, and watched through the corner of her eye, as Michael carefully marked a large cross in the very centre of her left cheek. That done, he stood back, and then bent forward to come within less than a centimetre of the cross he had drawn; a perfect stage-kiss. He repeated the process, this time from a different angle, and did so again. Lin began to giggle:

"Shut up you, this is serious."

He launched himself one more time.

"I need to sort out which is the best approach to be sure of landing in the right place . . . OK, finished," he said. "I reckon head sideways, eyes in front is best."

"So, you reckon you're going to give her a smacker, do you?"

She would have to be told, he thought; she was sure to find out tomorrow. "Have done already," he said, "and tomorrow night, we're going to the pictures. That's the good news; the bad news is that Sonny is coming too."

"Well how the hell did you manage that, you great daft pusball?"

"She invited him, not me."

"That's no problem," Lin said. "I'll phone the girls."

"What for?"

"We can kidnap Sonny on his way to the cinema . . ." She moved to the telephone, "take him round Clare's and chain him to the bed; he'd like that."

"Don't think so Lin," said Michael, stopping her. "She wants him there. Treez is never going to allow anything that could be called a date."

"Try and get rid of him after the film then," Lin suggested, "that way you could take her to the burger bar or somewhere."

"Shake Sonny off when there's food to be had? You sure?"

"Well get him round here tomorrow afternoon and stuff him full of cakes and chocolates, then shove lots of popcorn and ice cream down him during the film, and with any luck by the time you come out, he'll be feeling so sick, he won't be able to wait to leave you alone."

"There's no limit to your imagination when it comes to arranging liaisons, is there?"

"I'm ever so pleased you're going out," she said. "That means me and Jimmy can have the living room tomorrow night."

"That'll be nice for you," said Michael; "you could ask him to show you his clutch technique."

"Ha ha," said Lin. "I'm going to call him now." She picked up the phone and began to dial.

"Snog, snog, snog, snog. Snog, snog, snog, snog," Michael sang, on his way out of the door and up the stairs.

Roland chewed thoughtfully on his chocolate biscuit, while on the bench next to him, James sat with Lin on his

119

lap, doing something rather similar. Roland offered them both a piece of his biscuit, but it was no surprise to him that neither of them was interested.

"What I like about break," said Roland, "is it's a chance to sit and have a talk with your mates."

"Definitely, Sonny. Definitely," said James, staring into Lin's eyes.

"Alright, Jimmy, you can put me down now."

"Woof woof," said James, as she clambered over to sit between him and Roland.

"Looking forward to tonight then, Sonny?" Lin asked.

"Yeah," said Roland, "it's ages since Micky and me went to the pics. You remember Jimmy; one of us used to pay to get in, and then let the others in by the side exit."

"I remember it was usually me who wound up paying."

"We gave you money."

"Mike did, sometimes. You never. That was one of the reasons I stopped going with you. Not the main reason though," he said, kissing Lin on the end of her nose.

"Do you remember the first time you took me?" Lin asked James.

"How could I forget? They wouldn't let you into the dirty film, said you were too young. We had to see *Cinderella*, didn't we?"

"I thought it was lovely," said Lin.

"I didn't," said James. "I'd already been dragged kicking and screaming to see it when I was six, and I didn't like it then either."

"Well, you should have gone to see your sex film then. I wouldn't have stopped you."

"It was what you did stop me doing that I was worried about," he said.

120

"Why? You weren't going to do anything to a sweet little girl like me, were you?"

"Course not."

"You lying swine."

"Oh look." James noticed the approach of two familiar faces. "We're honoured today."

Michael and Theresa came over to sit with the other three.

"It's raining," Theresa explained.

"I wondered why you two would desert your gropers' gable," said James.

"We like to sit and discuss questions such as the meaning of life," said Michael, "something neither of us could profitably attempt with you."

"How do you know? I'm cheap, I am," James claimed.

"Thick, you mean?" Michael suggested.

"Come on then, ask me something," James said.

"Take it away, professor." Michael invited Theresa to pose one of her heavy questions.

"Alright then," said Theresa, "what about predestination?"

"Come again?" James looked blank.

"See," said Michael.

"No," Theresa held Michael back, "you didn't know what it meant either."

"A-ha." James sneered.

"It's fate," Theresa explained. "Are we all destined to follow certain paths in life, or are we free agents who can influence how our futures will develop?"

James thought. "You know, that's a very good question."

"So how about an answer then?" Michael demanded.

"Don't know."

"See what I mean? Thick!"

"No, hang on," said James; "I don't mean don't know

121

as in don't understand. I mean I can't prove whether it's true one way or the other, can I?"

"Actually, that is a good answer," said Theresa.

"See," said James.

"Wanna know what I think?" Roland asked.

"No!" Michael and James shouted simultaneously.

"Well," said Roland, "the way I look at it, is that the world, right, is in fact a spaceship, built by the squirrels."

"Squirrels?" Michael exclaimed, "those mangy little grey fleabags?"

"Yeah, squirrels," said Roland, "highly intelligent life-forms from another dimension, that disguise themselves as mangy little grey fleabags, to stop anyone finding out about them."

"So how come you know then?" James asked.

"Tarquin told me."

"Who's Tarquin?" Lin asked.

"Tarquin's my friend. He's a squirrel."

"And you're an idiot," Mike suggested.

Just a few weeks ago, Michael would have dived in to join the insane line of thought Roland wanted to start. Not any more.

"Tarquin says that they've got these transmitters built into the branches," Roland continued, "which they use to control humans. They sit inside the trees in special control rooms, where they keep us all under surveillance, all the time."

"Yes," said Theresa, straight-faced, "but won't all the acorns get in the way?"

"Acorns?" Roland gave her a strange look.

"Yes." Theresa was not going to be put off. "Squirrels eat acorns, and they store them inside trees."

"Squirrels eat acorns?" Roland scoffed. "Are you being stupid or what?"

"What do they eat then?" Theresa asked. Michael sighed. She had no idea what she was getting herself into here, he thought. Roland could reduce anyone's brain to custard in under fifteen minutes, given the chance.

"Penguins." Roland said it as if this was something everyone knew.

"So where do they find penguins in this country then?" Theresa demanded, taking him totally seriously.

"Tesco's." Roland said it as if this was something everyone knew.

"Tesco's don't sell penguins, though," said James.

"Yes they do," said Roland, "in packs of six, covered in chocolate." Roland offered James a piece of one again. He still didn't want any.

That was it for James. Any more of it and he would be burbling. Theresa wanted to carry on. She wanted to talk about the significance of chocolate biscuits in a post-industrial society. She didn't get the chance, because just then the bell sounded.

"Argh. Maths," said Lin. "Come on Sonny; sit next to me in the lesson, so that I can copy your wrong answers, and you can copy mine."

"Well, peasants," Michael announced, "I've got a free double period before lunch, so I'm off home."

"What if the prefect on duty sees you?" Theresa was becoming worried about Michael's truancy.

"I am the prefect on duty." Michael flashed his badge from behind his lapel. "If I catch myself, I promise to beat me up."

"What you got now Treez?" Lin asked, picking her things up.

"Sociology."

"What's that like then?" James asked, sliding out from the corner.

"It's better than working."

"I should have done that instead of Economics," said James. "I am not looking forward to this next hour."

When they all got out of the common room, Lin and Roland headed off to the Maths block, whilst Michael sneaked out of a side-door to make his way home. That left James and Theresa to walk together to the SocSci block.

"Sonny's ever so funny, isn't he?"

"Oh he's great fun," James agreed. "Trouble is, he's like that all the time. But then I expect you'll find that out tonight."

"It's a serious film," she said, "I wonder if he'll enjoy it?"

"Why did you want him to come?"

"He's a friend." Theresa was very defensive.

James wasn't buying that. "Come on Treez, do me a favour. I might not be up on philosophy or economics, but I can see what's going on."

Theresa surrendered. "I don't want Micky to think that I'm 'his' girl. I'm not anybody's property."

"And you think he's going to jump on you, if you give him half a chance?"

"No." Theresa felt uneasy with the way James looked at her.

"I'd jump on you," James said, nudging her, "if you asked me nicely."

"I don't think that's very likely."

"I know what you think," said James, "you think I only see you as a sex object, don't you?"

"I think you're only interested in me for that reason, same as you are with any girl."

"That's my reputation, I know. I wonder what it would take to live that down?"

124

"How about a year's total abstinence from all physical contact with the opposite sex?"

"No, I've got a better idea," he said. "Let me prove to you that I respect you: you come to bed with me, and I promise I shan't so much as touch you . . . if you don't want. What about that?"

"What about if you stopped sexually harassing me, Jimmy?" Theresa shouted, stopping in her tracks.

"I'm sorry. I only meant it in fun."

"What you meant is your problem." Theresa stepped briskly in the direction of her lesson. "My problem is that I can never feel at ease while you're around. Have you thought about that?"

"Oh come on . . ." James tried to keep up with her, "you don't think that I'm . . ." but Theresa had had more than enough.

"I don't know whether this Superstud act of yours is designed to impress your mates, or the girls, or both, or to fool yourself. I just wish you'd cut the crap with me, that's all!"

James watched as she marched off down the corridor. You aren't half sexy when you're angry, he thought of calling, but it didn't seem a very good idea.

"What's the matter, Jimmy?" Lin was sitting on James's lap on the sofa.

"Nothing." James dropped his arms from her sides. "Can you not do that?"

"I thought you liked it." Lin kept on rubbing his shoulders.

He shook his head. "Off," he said.

"Alright then." Lin stretched out on the sofa, and laid her head against his chest. She held him there still for a

125

while, quite contented. "Do you want a drink?" she asked.

"No thanks."

"Well I do," she said. "Hang on a minute."

Lin got up and went out to the kitchen, where her mother stood, ironing, with only the portable television for company.

"Everything alright?" June asked.

"Fine." Lin poured some water into a glass. "Ever so thirsty", she said, and headed back to the living room.

"You sure you don't want one?" said Lin, carefully transferring the water into one of the crystal tumblers from the drinks cabinet. James said nothing. Lin poured a double measure of vodka into her glass, and topped the bottle up with the water before closing the cabinet. She took a sip, and went back to rest her head upon him again.

"Lin," he said, softly stroking her hair at the back, "am I always making remarks? You know, trying it on?"

"Not always." James was relieved to hear that. "Just most of the time," she said.

"Really?" He felt quite put out.

"Of course, stupid."

"And do I brag and boast about girls a lot as well?"

"Yes. That's what you do when you're not making saucy remarks."

"Do you mind?" James was getting more and more worried.

"Well, yes and no . . ." Lin was becoming uncomfortable with this line of questioning.

"What do you mean?" James was seriously worried. He had never seen girls before as anything but nice soft lumpy things. He knew they had minds, but he never worried his own much about that. They came in different shapes, sizes and colours, and he adored them all. They were a bit like cream cakes, in fact. Not any more, though. He was so shocked, he had almost completely forgotten about the reason they were on the sofa in the first place.

Lin was getting fed up. "I don't want to talk about this, Jimmy." She toyed with the buttons on his shirt.

"Well I do," James said. "What do I do that annoys you?"

How about what you're doing now, she muttered under her breath. "Well . . ." Lin was hoping he would leave the subject if she gave him some answers, "it's not nice when you brag about girls behind their backs, is it? I mean, you know that was why Polly gave you the elbow, don't you?"

"I thought that was because of the girl at the party?"

"No, she only found out about that afterwards. That's another reason why . . ."

"I know."

"That's why I wouldn't have anything to do with you. Until you told me you were going to change."

"And you believed me?"

He was so intent on the conversation he hadn't even bothered to put his hand back on her bum when she had moved. She thought he must be ill or something. "Yes. Look, stop it will you, I don't want to go into all this."

"Alright then," said James. "Yes and no, you said, that means there must be things you particularly like about me. What are they?"

"Well . . ." Lin shifted her head and poked her fingers between his shirt buttons. She thought for a while. "Well," she said again. She poked about some more, and thought some more. "Well I don't know really," she said.

"Oh thanks."

127

"Hang on." She picked up her glass and took a gulp. She felt it go down. "Aaaah." She gasped for air.

"Well?" James awaited some compliment.

She thought again: "You've got a nice pair of boys' boobies," she said, moving her hand right under his shirt.

"Is that all?" It wasn't much of a compliment, he thought. Not for anyone, he thought. He thought of Theresa in the corridor, and saw what she had been getting at. It wasn't just a bit of fun. It was offensive.

"You're ever so good to me," said Lin.

That sounded a lot better. He held her closer.

Theresa, Michael and Roland emerged from the cinema into the cold night air.

"I thought that was good," said Theresa. "Did you?" she asked Michael.

"Yeah. Very good." Michael had found it hard to follow the film. His concentration had been spoilt by Roland scrunching popcorn and slurping orange all through it. If he was sick, Michael thought, it would only be proper punishment.

"I'm hungry," said Roland. "Can we go somewhere?"

"How about the burger bar, then?" Michael suggested, thinking that was sure to send him running for the gutter.

"Alright then," said Theresa, and they set off for the other end of the High Street.

"Isn't it quiet, with all the shops shut?" Theresa said.

"Quiet?" Michael said, "of course it's quiet; what do you expect in a graveyard?" He looked at all the shops. "Westone," he said. "West-Town; west of what?"

"Westone," said Roland, dramatically. "The mean streets. The police sirens. The drug-crazed Puerto Rican street gangs."

"The drug-crazed Puerto Ricans moved out ages ago," said Michael. "They couldn't keep up with the rising ghetto prices in the tree-lined, semi-detached suburban Georgian-effect slums you get around here."

"My parents moved here because they thought it would be a better place for us to grow up in," Theresa said.

"It's totally dead around here! Where could be worse?" Michael demanded.

"The moons of Pluto?" Roland suggested.

"Probably more going on there," Michael supposed.

"Yeah, but not such a nice atmosphere," said Roland.

Theresa wanted to make conversation. "I was born in London."

"Same as me," said Roland.

"Move down here to get away from people like him, did you?" Michael suggested.

"Yes, I suppose so."

"Ow." Roland was quite hurt by that one.

"Dad was very disappointed when they abolished the grammar schools. I was nearly sent private."

"Cripes, Ter-ai-ser," said Michael, "I bet you weren't half browned off when you learned you had to muck in with us rotters instead?"

"Gosh, yes," she said. "Frightful bunch of oiks."

Michael thought about that last remark of Theresa's. He wondered why thousands of kids read tons of rubbish about creatures from another planet who claimed to be schoolkids. They were ever so well-behaved, and always had jam for tea; or else they were stuck-up brats in boarding schools; or else they were skag kids on the dole; or else they were coping with parents who were divorced, dead, or gone to live in New Zealand, or all three; or else they were champion tennis-players, or if all else failed, they were American. Michael wondered why nobody was interested in what it was really like in the real world; where people go to normal schools, have normal parents, don't all have boyfriends and girlfriends and don't talk all the time as if they were absolutely certain who they were and what they were all about. Where were the real people, Michael wondered? They were invisible, he concluded, because they came from Westone!

"I don't come from round here!" Roland protested, insulted by the suggestion.

"No one comes from around here, except me!" Michael protested. "You're East End, she's West End, and McGarvey's a complete savage; he was born in some cave in Lancashire his Jock ancestors crawled to in the thirties."

"Don't forget Polly," added Theresa; "she's Liverpool-Irish, originally; and Zed's a Brummie."

"How come everyone round here comes from somewhere else?" Roland asked.

"They all got lost on the M25," said Michael, approaching the entrance to the burger bar, "and this is where they finally ran out of petrol."

"I'll just have some chips and a drink," said Theresa, as they stood in the queue, waiting to be served.

"Same here," said Michael.

"Well I'm not," said Roland. "I want a double cheeseburger, a large chips, and . . ."

"Hang on a minute, Sonny," said Michael. "Can we first establish the question of whether you have the means to pay for this?"

Roland pulled his baby-seal-on-the-ice face. Michael wished for a moment that he had a baseball bat.

"Have you actually got any money at all?" Theresa asked.

Roland dug into his pocket. "Thirtyeight pence," he said, showing it.

"Alright then, give it here." Michael snatched Roland's change.

"What about my bus fare?" Roland asked.

Michael slammed the money back into Roland's hand, and considered what was left. "Threepence," he said. "Wow."

They reached the front of the queue.

"What shall we do?" Theresa looked at Michael, with Roland looking at them both. "Shall we go halves?" she suggested. "I could pay for us all, I don't mind."

Michael decided what he was going to do: "Sorry," he said to the girl behind the counter. "We'll be back in a minute."

"What are we out here for?" Theresa stood with Michael outside the entrance, with Roland pressing his face against the glass on the inside.

"It's him, isn't it!" Michael protested, ordering Roland through the glass to get back and sit down. "He's had free entry to the pictures; drinks, sweets, the lot. Let's leave him and go somewhere on our own, eh?"

"Listen, Micky, if I want to pay for Sonny, then I will pay for him, OK?"

"So buy him something, and then we can push off."

"Now hang on a minute! I am not yours to push around and order about, like you do with him. Got that?"

"I know." Michael thought Miss Bossy Boots had too much of it. "You're a free agent. You do what you like.

You buy him so many cheeseburgers that he turns into Ronald Mc-bleeding-Donald if you want."

"I will!" Theresa raised her voice. "If I want!"

"And I shall buy my chips," said Michael. "Yeah, I shall buy my "takeaway" chips, and I shall sodding well take them away with me! Because I'm a free agent too, and I can go wherever I choose . . . Or wherever fate directs me . . . Or wherever the bleeding squirrels tell me to. Wherever. Alright!"

"You can go if you want," said Theresa, much quieter.

"I know I can. I don't need you to tell me that," Michael shouted. "I don't need your permission, your approval, your consent, for anything I do," he said, "except where it concerns you. And as far as doing anything that concerns you is concerned, well, it doesn't concern me, does it? OK!"

Michael turned his back on Theresa, and walked away, as far as the nearest lamp-post. He stood under it, propped against it with his out-stretched arms.

"Micky."

He had her feeling sorry for him now, but only because she could see that it wasn't an act.

"What?" Michael shouted, keeping his back to her.

"Are you crying?"

"Of course I'm not bloody crying!" he said, sniffling.

Rather uncertainly, she crept up to his lamp-post. "You are crying," she said.

"No I'm not!" He still tried to conceal his face.

Theresa could see him fighting a losing battle with his runny nose. "Oh Micky, I don't know how to handle this." She looked across the road for some kind of inspiration, or escape. Her attention focused on the lamp-post opposite. She ran to it, and hid herself behind it, all the while trying to think of the right thing to say.

Inside the burger bar, Roland watched them both through the window, and wondered why all this was necessary to sort out who was buying his cheeseburger.

"That stuff about boys not crying," Theresa called from her hiding-place, thinking hard, "it's only a form of sex-role stereotyping." Skip the Sociology, she thought; speak English. "It's all crap!" she shouted. She couldn't hear any sound from Michael. She thought she had better carry on. "It's the same as saying that women don't sweat!" she called. She tried to think of another example. "Or don't have hairy arms!" she suggested, not very eruditely. "Well I'll tell you something!" she called, "I sweat buckets, I do. And I've got ever such hairy arms!" She waited a while, but there was no response. She wondered if he could hear her properly.

"I'm the best cook in our house!" Michael called back, eventually.

"Well there you are!" Theresa hollered, relieved, "all I can cook is scrambled eggs or omelette; and then I don't know which it's going to be until I've finished! Your turn!"

"I used to play with Lin's dolls!" Michael shouted, honestly.

"I used to play with Gordon's racing cars!" she cried back.

"I sometimes wear a bra and suspenders!" Michael shouted, very loudly, so that a couple of passing pedestrians could hear.

Theresa tried to follow that. "I have to shave twice a day since I had my vasectomy!" she hollered.

Theresa came out from her hiding-place and walked across to Michael. "Can I buy you a drink?" she asked him, leaning on his lamp-post.

"Here you are." Michael handed Roland a cheeseburger, chips and a chocolate milk-shake. "From each according to his abilities, to each according to his gob-size. Karl Marx."

"Thanks Micky." Roland began tucking in.

"Save the bag; you might need it later on to throw up in." Roland took a large bite out of the cheeseburger and chewed contentedly.

"I'll see you tomorrow, Sonny, OK?" Roland nodded, and mumbled something incomprehensible with his mouth full. "Treez says bye bye too." Michael could see a smear of sauce and fragments of lettuce were trying to escape from the side of Roland's mouth. He felt ill just watching. He picked up his chips and left.

"Where are we going?" Michael asked Theresa who was standing outside, handing her a bag of chips.

"I know a place," she said.

"So," said Michael, "this is the famous Argie pub."

"You mean you haven't been here before?" Theresa asked, reaching the bar.

"No fear," he said. "It's always full of those potty Chimp-Pack girls."

"Well I can't see any in tonight. What do you want?"

"Nuclear disarmament and an end to famine in the Third World? How about you?"

"To drink," she said.

Without knowing it, they sat down in James and Lin's Quiet Corner.

"Well, here's to you, Mrs Robinson." Michael raised his glass.

"Cheers." Theresa took a sip of her wine.

"That was a good film, *The Graduate*," Michael said. "Saw it on telly last week."

"I thought it was sexist."

She thought that about everything, Michael thought.

"Well what did you think of the chips, then?" Michael said, changing the subject, daring her to find them sexist.

"Lacking in substance. Entertaining, but with no serious message, I thought."

"We could go to the fish and chip shop next time if you like? The chips there are really heavy with social realism."

They had done all the families and favourite records stuff back on their bench, but it was obvious to Michael that they still hardly knew anything about each other. He knew he wanted to know more. Everything. All about the girl, he thought.

"Next time?" It had been going very well, she thought. They had gone out, and now they were talking and having a drink. This was good. But now he was showing signs of ambition, it looked like. He wanted dates, and probably all-in wrestling as well, she supposed, and she wasn't at all sure she wanted that. Not even with this one. Not yet.

"If you want," he said. "Wherever you want."

She tried to make it sound polite. "I don't go out a lot, Micky. I could never be like Lin; in here two or three times every week."

"That's only temporary; until she gets a supply of booze plumbed into the bathroom."

"I've got lots of work to do."

"So have I," said Michael. "Sometimes I even do some of it."

"You should take your studies more seriously."

"Studying I take seriously, it's teachers I can't take seriously. I read the books, follow the course, but I'm not going to spend any more time than I have to on a load of stupid exercises," he said, taking a mouthful of lager.

"You sound just like my brother."

"What? The married one, or the one in prison at university?"

"The one in prison."

"Well, there you are then. Didn't do him any harm, did it?"

"Dad says he could have gone to Cambridge, if he'd tried."

"What do I want to go to Cambridge for, except to change trains for Harwich and the Continent?"

"Do you know where you'll go when you leave school?"

"Home, probably."

"But what's your ambition?" Theresa kept trying to get a serious answer out of him, not knowing when she had.

"To save the world," Michael declared, with immaculate sincerity. She thought he was joking.

"I want to study Literature and Philosophy," she said.

"Why?"

"So that I can answer that question. And I want to go around the world, by bus."

"You'd get wet."

"India I want to see, and China, and South America."

"Great Yarmouth, Marbella, Land's End, Great Yarmouth," said Michael, meaningfully.

"What's that?"

"That's the furthest I've ever been; North, South, East and West."

"Oh. Lanzarote," she said.

"North, South, East or West?"

"South and West."

"What about North and East?"

"Here, I think," she admitted, reluctantly.

"I could show you Great Yarmouth one day if you like? It's on the way to China."

"Ah, the exotic East. Mysterious Norfolk." She drank some wine. "We're supposed to be the lucky ones, living in a place like this."

"As we used to say in biology: the other male humanoid's blade-leafed herbage always contains a greater concentration of chloroplasts."

"Comprehensive education's a wonderful thing." She drank to it.

"It's like what Gandhi said about Western Civilisation," Michael responded, "it would be a good idea."

More than half-way through his drink, Michael was at that magic moment for him when he had stopped being cynical but had not yet become totally incoherent. "It's like with the books in the library," he continued, "I reckon it's all part of an enormous system that wants to take away our identity; tells us that what we know doesn't exist, to make us believe the Lie."

"What's the Lie?"

"Trust Authority," said Michael. "The Lie says that they know what they're talking about, and they don't."

"The older generation have given us two world wars and the destruction of the Earth's resources," said Theresa. "I know when not to believe them."

"It's not anybody's generation," Michael explained. "Our generation's just as full of idiots who'll be the death of us as any other. We had two world wars because too many people believed the Lie, and

137

we'll kill the whole planet if we carry on believing it."

"Who invented the Lie in the first place, then?"

"The Lie's always existed, waiting around for people to come along and believe it. You find the Lie in governments, families . . . religions . . . schools! Anywhere they tell you that your conscience is wrong. Anywhere they tell you they know best, and make it a crime for you to disagree."

She thought that made sense. "I really enjoy talking with you, Micky," she said.

"I suppose you know," Michael said, hesitatingly, "I'd like to be doing more than talking?" He reached out and held her hand, and began gently stroking her fingers.

"Stop it." She took her hand away. She started to gaze downwards and looked into the reflection in her wineglass. "Sometimes I wonder what it's like. Sex," she said.

"Hey." He thought she had misunderstood him, "I didn't mean . . ."

"I know," she said. "I don't just mean penetration," she said, with brutal accuracy, just like a doctor's daughter. "I mean being sexual with someone." She gave a nervous chuckle. "Not something I know a great deal about." She watched the colours on the rim of her glass. She wanted to be more open with him, but couldn't bring herself to do it.

"Do you fantasise?" Michael was oblique. He was unable to come right out with what he wanted to say, but hoped she would catch his meaning.

"How do you mean?" She had missed his drift.

"Imagine you're with someone," he said. "Someone you know."

"Is that what you do then?" She thought he just meant

138

dreaming about someone. She knew all about boys' wet dreams, in theory, but did not make the connection with what Michael was telling her now.

"All the time," he admitted, laughing.

"Anyone I know?" she asked.

"Everyone." He took a drink, feeling a lot less tense now he'd finally told someone about it. "Some a lot more than others."

"Who are they?" she enquired, not sure that she should.

"Never you mind," he said, wryly.

"But I've been in there, have I?" she suggested, still thinking of soft cuddly dreams, not what he was talking about at all.

"Yeah," he admitted, nervously, not realising that she didn't fully understand what he was actually talking about.

"I've never thought of it like that," she said. "Not faces. Not even particular, well, bodies." She struggled to find the words. "Just the idea of it all, and what it would be like."

"Do you like the idea of it?"

"The idea? Yes. Sometimes. But sometimes I think of this strange picture: it's like I'm looking over the edge of a rock by the sea, and there's lots of people in the water. Some of them are swimming, some just floating; and they're all shouting at me to come in. 'The water's lovely,' they say. But from where I am, on the rock, I can see other people, further out, and they look as if they want to swim back, but they can't. And some of them keep going under. And I'm thinking: they might not come up again. And once they go in the water, nobody ever comes back out." Theresa felt somewhat embarrassed at having described the dream-sequence: "Do you understand?"

Michael put on a silly voice: "Ya, iss bekaus you vont to return to ze security off zer voomb. But ziss iss impossible, you see, bekaus you vould not fit back in zere, you see."

"Do you want another drink?" She was smiling warmly at him. She thought they were getting through to each other, in a funny sort of way.

Michael looked at his glass. "I've barely half-finished this one," he said, "but you're nearly as much of an alkie as my Sis, by the look of it."

Theresa looked at her glass, not realising that she had sipped her way to the bottom of it.

"Shall I get you another?" Michael offered.

"Orange juice," she said.

"Here comes my bus." Theresa looked out from the shelter. She turned to where Michael was standing. "Well, thanks for waiting with me," she said, "and for the whole evening. I've enjoyed it."

"Me too," said Michael. "Thanks."

The bus pulled up at the stop. Michael checked to see if his father was driving. He wasn't.

"Well, bye then." Theresa climbed the first step onto the bus.

"Hang on . . ." Michael climbed onto the step with her. Oh no, he thought. You don't get away that easy. Not this time.

"Micky?"

He grabbed her round the middle, and before she knew what was happening he was kissing her. She made a noise that sounded like a protest, and he backed off.

For a while they looked at each other, speechless. "See you tomorrow," he muttered, and climbed down from the step. The doors closed, and she was carried off.

He crossed the road, and waited for his bus, replaying what had just happened in his mind, over and over again.

"Well?" said Lin, opening the door. "What happened?"

"We went to the cinema," said Michael.

"I know that, but what happened? Did you take Sonny to the burger bar?"

"Yes." Michael hung up his coat. Here we go, he thought. Interrogation Time.

"And did you leave him there, and go somewhere on your own with Treez?" Lin eagerly demanded to know the details. This was a big moment for her. She had been getting worried about him. Afraid he'd cock it up, again.

"Yes we did."

"Where? The Argie Pub?"

"That's the place."

"And?"

"And we had a drink," said Michael, making for the living room.

"And what happened?" Lin demanded, following him in. "Oh come on, tell me. I told you about me and Jimmy."

Michael only smiled and raised his eyebrows at her.

"I know what happened," she said, "you and her got off together, didn't you?"

"No, we did not get off together," said Michael, sitting down.

"Yes you did," she taunted him.

"No we didn't," he said. "The only thing we got off was the bus."

"Well what happened, then?"

He thought about what had happened, and how much of it he might be able to explain to her. He decided not to try.

Chapter 5

There was never anything much to do in the mornings over half-term. Lin often found this situation quite frustrating, but Michael thought he could probably handle it.

"What you doing?" Lin wandered in on Michael in the living room, searching for something of interest.

"I'm in training for the Olympics." Michael was slouched on the sofa, watching the children's programmes on television.

"You'd die of exhaustion if you tried to run a bath," said Lin, prowling around the room, like a cat in a cage.

"The television coverage," said Michael. "I'm going to have to sit like this for about eleven hours a day during the summer. I'm not sure I'll be able to take it."

"You managed alright when all that stupid football was on last year."

"All that stupid football!" Michael berated her. "That was the World Cup! The most important event in all civilisation . . . and Scotland." Michael chuckled. "Ha ha! Weren't half good, having McGarvey round here to see his ancestors making complete pratts of themselves, live in front of 900 million people."

"Football's stupid," said Lin. "You should be thinking about more important things."

"Like what? Exams?" Michael hated her when she tried to be his other mum.

"Like your birthday," she said. "Your Eighteenth Birthday." Michael eighteen? It didn't sound right. She looked at him, sitting there, enthralled by the puppets intended for tiny tots, and wondered whether there might have been some mistake on the birth certificate. "I'm the one who should be coming of age, not you," she said.

"You?" Michael thought that sounded rich.

"Yeah, me. The mature one around here," Lin declared.

"The only time you've ever been mature," Michael said, "is when you were full of Dad's twelve year old Scotch."

Lin's mood changed: "You had some too." She leant over the back of the sofa, trying to grab him in an arm-lock.

"Not as much as you, though," he said, knowingly, fending her off.

Some three years earlier, when their parents had left them to go on holiday alone, thinking they were finally old enough to be trusted, Michael and Lin had got drunk together. Lin particularly so. Michael, having been left in charge of both the house and the baby sister, had, by himself, to glue the broken ornaments back together, explain all the screaming in the garden to the neighbours, buy a new bottle of best malt out of the housekeeping he had been left, and clean up the mess in the bathroom and on the stairs, despite the fact that it wasn't his. The experience had been enough to put him off drink altogether, until tempted back very recently by the arrival on the doorstep of James bearing multipacks of lager. For Lin, the effect had been quite different, a bit like introducing a tramp to meths.

"I wonder if anyone will get like that at your party?"

"Party? Who says I'm having a party?"

"Of course you're having a party; it's your Eighteenth. You've got to."

"Oh. In The Rules, is it?"

143

"Yeah." She thought now would be as good a time as any to tell him. "Plus I've already invited a few people," she said.

"You've invited people to my party that I didn't even know I was having?" Michael did not sound pleased.

"Only a few."

"Who?"

"No one much; only Polly, Clare, Jill, Zed . . ." He didn't let her go on.

"I'm having a party I don't know about, and I'm having all of your Hyena-Pack friends to it, am I?"

"Brownie Pack."

Despite what he said, Michael did want a party, but he would have liked to be in rather more charge of the arrangements than Lin was likely to allow.

"I could ask Jimmy to come as well," she said, as if offering a great favour to him.

"I bet you could, and I bet I know why."

"I haven't seen Sonny yet, though, and I thought I should leave you to ask Treez."

"That's ever so considerate of you, Lin. You're so good to me."

"In fact there's only a couple more people you'll need to see about it."

"Who's that?"

"Mum and Dad."

That did it. That was enough, Michael thought. "You're going in the dustbin, you are," he said. He got up and pulled her legs from under her.

"Oh Micky, no. No don't . . . Stop it! Let go!"

"Hi Jim," said Michael, walking down the drive, carrying Lin like a sack of coal.

144

"Jimmy. Help!"

James understood very well what was going on here, being a fully paid up member of the Big Brothers' Union himself. "Nah. Mike doesn't look like he needs any help."

Michael knocked the lid off one of the dustbins. "What's in there?" Lin sounded worried.

"Nothing, yet," Michael said.

Lin had been going in the dustbin for many years, whenever Michael decided that she was being particularly annoying. When she was smaller, Michael used to put her all the way in, put the lid on, and sit on top. She used to scream her head off when this happened, and Michael got hit more than once by Phil because of it. Eventually, she got too big to go right in, and Michael learned not to do it unless the bin was empty. She was still liable to go in, though, but Michael was finding it more and more difficult to get her there.

Struggling desperately, Lin managed to kick the bin over onto its side. "Give us a hand, Jim." James picked up the dustbin, and held it for Michael as he forced Lin into it backwards, pushing her down so far that she could never get out unaided.

"You beasts! I hate both of you!" Lin shouted with her chin between her knees.

"When do the bin men come?" James asked.

"They've already come this morning, unfortunately," said Michael.

"Get me out of here Jimmy. Now!"

"Please," James prompted her.

"Please," she said, and James went to lift her out.

"Well, Jimbo, there's no one else home, so if you two want to be alone . . ." Lin hit Michael when she got back on her feet. "Can't think why," he said.

"No," said James, "I can think of something much more interesting than that." Lin looked very hurt by the boys adding insults to injury. "Phone Sonny," said James. "Tell him to get round here."

"Why?" Michael asked.

"You'll find out," said James. "When he comes."

James sat by the window, waiting for Roland to make an appearance at the end of the road.

"What is it?" Michael asked. "Has he had a leg-extension or something?"

"Just you wait and see," said James. "Little pillock better bring it, that's all."

"Bring what?" Lin asked.

"Here he is," James cried. "Have a look."

Lin and Michael came to the window, and saw what all the fuss was about.

"I don't believe it," said Michael. "It shouldn't be allowed."

"It isn't," said James, "but that doesn't stop him."

"Where did he get it from?" Lin wondered.

"Come on," said James, "let's go and have a proper look."

Roland pulled off his crash-helmet and saw the three of them coming towards him. "Hi, Fans," he said, switching the engine off.

"Is it a proper motorbike?" Lin asked.

Michael studied it. "No; it's a self-propelled hair-drier."

"It's only a moped," Roland explained. "It's restricted, but it'll do sixty . . . over a cliff."

"So where did you steal this from, then?" James asked.

146

"I never stole it. It's me brother's. He stole it." Michael really didn't know whether Roland was joking or not.

"I saw this coming down the High Street yesterday," James told them. "I thought, well, either the circus is in town, advertising trick-riding midgets, or that's Sonny with a pair of wheels."

"Can you fit two on it?" Lin wondered.

"Easy."

Roland moved forward on the saddle, and Lin climbed aboard behind, hanging on to his shoulders. James showed her the proper way to hold on, around the waist. "Oh can we go for a ride?" she pleaded.

"No you can't," James told her. "It's illegal."

"It'd be alright," said Lin. "Only to the end of the road and back."

"He can't carry passengers," said Michael. "He's a learner."

Lin reached behind her, and then in front, ripping off Roland's L-plates, and throwing them on the drive. "No he's not," she said.

"You haven't got a helmet," said James.

"Yes she has," said Roland, passing her his. Lin put it on, without fastening the strap, and Roland kick-started the machine. They lurched off to the top of the cul-de-sac, veering all over the road. Reaching the end, Roland stalled. He started the engine again, and came back narrowly missing a couple of parked cars, with Lin waving her arms in the air throughout.

Michael was not impressed: "Get off that, you," he ordered, grabbing her under the arms, and dragging her over the back of the bike.

"You leave me alone," she shouted, from inside the full-face helmet.

"Lin." James knocked three times on her head to gain her

147

attention. She turned around. "Wait till I've got the car, eh?"

"Stop telling me what to do," she said, "I'm nearly as old as you."

"And take that thing off," said James. "You look like a used match."

"I'll wear it if I want," she said, stubbornly. "Alright Sonny?" Roland did not object. "Sonny and me," she said, "are having tea. You two can make your own." She marched huffily back to the house.

"Either of you know how to adjust the brakes on this?" Roland asked.

"Get the tools out," said James.

"Tools?" Roland looked blank. James looked under the saddle, to find that there were no tools.

"I'll open the garage," said Michael. "You go and tell Lin it's four teas," he said to Roland, "or she goes back in the bin."

"When's your driving test, then?" Michael asked James through the spokes of the front wheel.

"Next week." James sounded less than confident.

"You'd better not fail it." Lin was sitting on the saddle, holding the handlebars, and still wearing Roland's helmet. "You're taking me to the seaside, remember?"

"It's nearly November, you stupid daft cow," said Michael, holding the wheel in place. Lin turned the key in the ignition and sounded the horn. It was right next to Michael's ear. He jumped. She laughed.

"This tea is disgusting," said James, painfully swallowing a mouthful, and pouring what was left down the drain.

"I make nice tea," Lin protested. "I'm trained."

"So are the monkeys on television," said Michael, "and they can't make it either."

Lin twisted the throttle on the bike. "I'm going to get one of these, so's I can run you over with it."

"I wouldn't bank on me passing this time," said James, tightening the brake-cable. "We might have to make it a trip to London for the Christmas lights instead."

"Christmas!" Lin moaned. "That's ages. Take me to the seaside, Sonny. We can go tomorrow."

"You do, and I'll tell Dad," Michael warned her.

"Don't worry," said James. "This pile of junk wouldn't make it to the by-pass."

"Not with him in control, it wouldn't," Michael suggested.

"Well, Micky," said Lin; "are you going to tell them, or shall I?"

"Tell them what?" Michael was not paying much attention to her. He might have discovered girls, now, but motorbikes were still more interesting than sister creatures.

"Micky is having a party for his Eighteenth," Lin announced. "Lots of sex, drugs and funky music; and you're all invited."

"Have we got to buy him presents?" Roland asked.

"Yes," Michael said. "Expensive ones."

"I'll buy you a drink, Mike, alright," said James.

"I'll draw you a picture," Roland offered.

"What shall I get?" Lin asked.

"Lost?" Michael suggested.

Back in school, the Awful Day came quickly for James. "Cheer up, Jimmy, you'll pass." Lin tried to get his attention out from behind his Highway Code. "He'll pass, won't he Treez?"

"Probably not," said Theresa, leaning against the school gates.

"Oh shut up!" Lin rounded angrily on Theresa.

"She's right," James muttered, quite defeatist about the whole thing.

"Loads of people fail the first time, especially young men, who tend to regard driving as some sort of test of their manhood." Theresa was quite enjoying getting some back on James, in a not too nasty sort of way.

"I can think of a much better way to test that." James nudged Theresa. He knew it annoyed her, but she had started it, he thought.

"You wouldn't be able to manage that either, if you had to pass a test first," said Theresa, curtly.

"That would depend on what the instructor looked like," James suggested.

"It wouldn't work like that," Theresa told him. "You'd have to stand under a spotlight, and simulate on video for a panel of doctors, magistrates and agony columnists, all women. You'd have to prove to them that you were considerate and responsible. Otherwise you'd have to keep wearing the chastity belt."

"I thought we didn't go in for all that sexual harassment?" James retorted.

"Just letting you know how it feels," she said.

"Here comes my lift." James spotted an approaching car.

"Good luck." Lin gave him a quick kiss.

"Thanks," said James, "I shall need it." The car pulled up. James opened the door and got into the passenger seat.

"Do you want the tip then?" Theresa asked, as he was shutting the door. He wound down the window to hear her: "The collected wisdom of two parents and two big brothers, passed on to me, in the hope that somebody in the family might pass first time one day; though my money's on my little niece."

"OK," said James. "What's the tip?"

Theresa recounted what she had been told. "Well, apparently, the trick is to go slower than everything else on the road, but only just; to wait all day, if necessary, for a space three times bigger than you need for a right turn; and don't just move your eyes to look in your mirrors, move your head as well, so you can be seen looking, even when you're not looking. It's not so much a driving test as a form of ritual hypocrisy, in which people proclaim their belief in things they have no intention of practising in later life."

"Sounds just like Father Ray's catechism," James said, "and I managed to bluff my way through that alright."

"Go on. Good luck," said Theresa.

"Thanks," said James. He would up the window, and the car drove off. Lin and Theresa turned and walked back into school.

"You like my Jimmy, don't you?"

"Don't start that again, Lin."

"No, I mean friendly-like, that's all."

"He's OK," said Theresa. "For a boy."

"But you can be really nasty to him, sometimes, can't you?"

"He started it," said Theresa. "Besides, you've got to be like that with your mates, or else they get the wrong idea."

"What?" Lin looked blank.

"Ask Micky. He'll explain."

"How are you and Micky getting on at the moment?" Lin kept asking her that one.

"Fine." Theresa kept giving that answer.

"Will you be going out with him again?"

"If there's something we both want to go to, I expect so."

"What about his party?"

"Yes, he's told me all about how you've hijacked that."

151

"I'm only helping him organise it. You are coming, aren't you?"

"Yes, I'm coming." Theresa wasn't entirely sure about that, but she thought it would look very rude if she said no. She could just tell when Lin was planning something.

"Oh," said Lin. "Good."

Lin was planning something.

After tea, Lin went looking for her brother. She found him in his room, reading one of his military weapons books.

"What d'you want for your birthday, Micky?" she asked from the doorway.

"A helicopter-gunship," said Michael, studying the data on one.

He hadn't shouted at her to go away, or thrown anything at her, so she reckoned it was safe to step inside. "How much are they?"

"About 14 million pounds."

"Can't afford it." She began checking through his music collection. "Will a new tape do?"

"Suppose so."

"It's going to be a really good night," she said. "We can clear the furniture out of the living room for dancing, Mum's going to do us some food, and she says we can have beer and wine, but no hard stuff."

"Bit of a blow for you, that?"

"I'll manage," said Lin. "Question is, what will you be doing?"

"Me? I thought I might open all my presents first," Michael said, lying back on his bed, "have a little drink before you tank the lot, not let any girls in unless they give me a kiss first."

"You can be a bit more ambitious than that on your

birthday, you know," she said, looking down at him.

"I wouldn't mind a smooch with Clare Hunter," said Michael, thoughtfully.

"Never mind about Clare," said Lin. "What about Treez?"

"Have a smooch with her too, with any luck."

"Skip the dancing Micky." She came to the point: "Are you going to get off with her? You do want to get off with her, don't you?"

"Get off with Treez?"

No, thought Lin, with next door's labrador! "Yes, get off with Treez. Get hold of her and give her a good snog?" She thought it was quite possible that he didn't know what it was. "You've never done it, have you?" she taunted.

"Yes I have," he declared, jeering back at her.

"Who with?" She certainly didn't believe him.

"I don't kiss and tell."

"Got nothing to tell, that's why," she said. "Come on. Who did you get off with, then?"

He gave in. "Karen Pearson," he said. The girl he mentioned was an extremely attractive Upper Sixth girl.

"Karen Pearson! You never." Lin was surprised, and not fully convinced.

"Did," Michael said, totally straight-faced.

"Seriously?"

"Yeah. Straight."

"You never said anything before," she said. "When was it?"

"Little while ago." He was beginning to sound un-convincing again, she thought.

"How little?" Lin didn't believe it. Karen Pearson? And him?

"Couple of years," he said, vaguely.

"Two years ago? In the Fifth Year, you mean?"

"Fourth Year."

"That's three years."

"Fourth Year, Juniors." The truth was finally out, he thought.

"What, when you were ten!" Lin exclaimed, feeling quite cheated. "That doesn't count."

"They're not that easy to find, you know. Real girls."

"Well you've found one now, haven't you?" Lin punched him playfully in the stomach.

"She won't." Michael sat down, his bravado having completely evaporated.

"Yes she will." Lin tried to encourage him. "You've just got to play it properly, that's all."

"The Famous Rules again?"

"Yes, and you know all that stuff by now, don't you? Don't you? You don't." She flung open the wardrobe, and threw him his coat. "Put that on," she said. "You're coming out with me."

The doorbell rang. June got up and went to answer it.

"Oh, hello James darling." She was a little surprised to see him.

"I've passed," he said, still not believing it himself. "I've actually passed."

"That's very good. Lin mentioned you were taking your test today."

"Where is she?"

June was confused. "Well, I thought they'd gone out with you, either to celebrate or drown your sorrows. Has there been some sort of mix-up over where you were supposed to meet, then?"

"Oh, no. I just came round expecting her to be here, that's all."

"Well they haven't been gone long. I'm sure you can catch them up, now that you're mobile. They said they were going to the Argie pub."

"Yes." James prepared to go and gloat and be showered with kisses.

"Only I hope you're not going to be planning on drinking if you're driving, young man?"

"No. I'm not that daft."

"Glad to hear it," said June, "not if you're going to be chauffeuring my girl around from now on. Now I can see her drinking and driving, one day."

Yes, thought James, both at the same time, probably. He said his goodbyes, and went in search of her.

"You didn't half look worried when that bus came," said Michael, following Lin to the Quiet Corner, "in case it was Dad."

"Well, it's the third time I've been in here since Saturday." Lin arrived at the table, carrying their wine. "I think he might be getting angry with me."

"You should cut down on the booze," said Michael, sitting opposite her.

"I'm going to, soon as me and Jimmy start going for drives together."

He watched her pour herself a very large glass of wine from the carafe. "But you'll carry on forcing yourself till then, will you?" he suggested.

"I want to get completely pissed out of my mind at your party," she said, taking her first taste of wine. "I won't have to worry about getting home for once."

"Do I get any of that?" Michael eyed the drink.

"Of course you do." She poured him a glass. "This'll help you to talk."

Michael watched her fill his glass to the rim: "You should get a job with the police, I reckon, with your interview technique."

"If you want to get off with Treez," said Lin, bluntly, "You're going to have to plan it."

"You're going to plan it, you mean?"

"What are little sisters for?"

"Forever, unfortunately. Friends, you can choose, relatives, you're stuck with."

"Do you want me to help or not?"

"Only teasing; that's what big brothers are for."

"Big brothers are for finding you boyfriends," said Lin, approvingly, "and you've done that for me, so now it's my turn."

"Alright then," said Michael, "go and get me Clare Hunter in a leopardskin leotard."

"Forget Clare. She is out of your league."

"How about Polly, then?"

"She'd eat you for breakfast."

That sounded nice, he thought. "I quite like Jill," he suggested.

"She doesn't like you."

"Little Zed keeps giving me looks?"

"She's strictly off limits," said Lin. "Her dad keeps a very close eye on her."

"That only leaves Whatsername then, don't it?" Michael said, trying to sound nonchalant.

Lin started to point at Michael and smile: "Don't give me that! You're soft for her. Your First Love!"

Watching from across the bar, James could see Michael and Lin talking together intently, like long-lost friends. He had never seen them like that before. Normally, he thought, they fought like ferrets in a sack, as his Grandad would have said. Should he go over to them? He decided it would do no harm to leave it for a day. They seemed to be very happy together, and it might not be the right thing to intrude. Besides, he thought, there was someone else he could go see.

"Excuse me, but do you know where they keep the dirty books around here?"

"There's plenty of stuff on soil under Geography," said Theresa, only glancing at him for an instant, "that dirty enough for you?" She resumed reading her book, as if he wasn't there.

"What are you doing?" He turned the page for her without asking.

"Work," she said, turning it back.

"You know what they say. All work and no play makes Treez a Girlie Swot?"

"All play and no work gets you on the YTS. You want to pass, you've got to put the hours in."

"Who says?" James reached inside his jacket, and produced an L-plate. He tore it into four, and threw the pieces onto Theresa's book.

"You got it?" She was now paying him some attention.

"Yep. And you know what? I owe it all to you."

"Go away," she said, and turned back to her book.

"No, really. I did everything you said, and it worked."

She was sticking doggedly to her book, but James did not give up easily. He sat on the table opposite her, making it plain that if she was staying, he was staying. "How much longer you planning to hang around here?" he asked.

"I've nearly finished my homework. I was just going to take these books down to the desk."

157

"Good timing by me, I thought, arriving when I did?"

"If you're offering me a lift home, Jimmy, then I would be very grateful."

"I'd be happy to take you home," said James, "but I could do even better than that for you."

"Jimmy, I think we know each other well enough to know the answer to that one." She closed her book and began getting ready to leave.

"In your dreams . . ." James began. Theresa winced. ". . . did you ever wish that a handsome prince would come along and sweep you off your feet, and carry you off to his enchanted kingdom?"

"No. Don't think so," she said.

"Good, because that's not going to happen tonight," said James, cheekily.

"Fairy tales are not only sexist, they're elitist," said Theresa. "If any princes come bothering me, I shall tell them to renounce their titles, establish democratic government in their kingdoms, give all their riches back to the people, and stop locking princesses up in towers."

"What I thought was that we could go for a little drive somewhere?"

"What for?" She thought she knew what for, knowing him.

"Does there have to be a reason?"

"For me to get in that car with you, and not know where I'm going, there has to be a pretty good reason, yes."

"We can go wherever you want to go."

"My house," she said, "by the most direct route possible."

"You want to go home now, you can get the bus," James replied, responding to her bluntness. "But you could take a chance on me, and let me prove to you that I'm not the mad rapist you seem to think I am. I'm sorry if I've said things that you thought were out of order. I never meant any harm. Please can we be friends?"

He had said his piece, and he waited for her reaction.

"Alright, let me take these books out first," she said.

Theresa had not expected a limousine or anything, but she was still unprepared for the sight that greeted her.

James wrenched the driver's door open. "Not much to look at, I know, but then I couldn't stand the competition, could I?"

"Where can we go?" She was thinking it had best be somewhere on a bus route, so that she could get back by herself, if necessary.

"You choose," he said. She got in, and struggled gamely with the seatbelt strap.

She finally managed to strap herself in. "OK go to the end of the by-pass, and I'll direct you from there."

"Now if I'd suggested we come here," said James, "you'd never have agreed."

"Why do you say that?" Theresa fought her way out of the seat-belt, and sat looking out through the windscreen.

"Oh come on, you do know why people come up here?"

From their vantage on top of the hill, Theresa could see the lights of Westone, flickering below them in the darkness. "For the view," she said.

"During the day, yes, but at night this is Lovers' Lookout. You poke around in the grass up here, and chances are you'll find somebody's lost virginity."

"I never knew." She was now feeling quite the fool.

"Fat lot of use sitting in that library's done you, hasn't it?"

"Alan used to bring Sandy up here before they were married," she said, seeing something familiar in a new perspective.

"We might get visited by the police if we're lucky," said James. "They'll ask you if you're over sixteen. Tell them no, but it's your birthday tomorrow, and we're waiting for midnight."

"Doing it in the back of a little tin box. I don't think I could imagine anything more squalid."

"I could," said James. "Have you seen the girls under the town hall clock at nights?"

"Are they . . .?" Theresa had never thought it possible.

"Working, yes," said James. Theresa felt even more foolish, and naive with it.

"They're down there now." She was picturing the scene.

"There's one who used to go to our school, I've noticed," said James. He wondered what sort of conclusions Lin might jump to, if he ever admitted noticing such things to her.

"They all went to somebody's school," said Theresa. "They're all somebody's daughters."

Pokey little commuter towns were never much to look at, or talk about, James thought, even when they were flickering in the moonlight. Above Westone, there was a whole universe on view at the moment. Much more interesting, he thought: "Do you think there's intelligent life on other planets?" he asked.

"I don't know, do you think there's intelligent life on this one?"

He wasn't corny, she thought; he was a grain mountain.

"There's You and Me," James said. She didn't respond. "I've not raped you yet, in case you haven't noticed."

"Me, I'm careful where I tread. No handsome boy will

160

ever leave me dead." Theresa spoke out loud what she was thinking. It was a line from a song about Marilyn Monroe, but James didn't know that. All he thought was this one is so deep, you'd need a diving board to get to the bottom of what she is thinking.

"So what's the situation between you and Mike?" James asked, returning to Earth.

"Micky's one of the few people in the world I call friend," she said, "along with Lin, my sister-in-law Sandy, and Nell."

"Who's Nell?" James thought he knew the name of every attractive girl at Warren Park, Our Lady and Westone Girls, but none of them were called Nell. He didn't want to let one slip by unnoticed.

"Nell Gwynne is my King Charles Spaniel." Theresa had seen what he was thinking, and didn't half enjoy disappointing him.

"What? Don't I even get in along with the dog?" James was put out.

"There may be some movement in the computer-rankings soon," Theresa admitted, "particularly after somebody chewed my best shoes. It was probably the dog. Definitely wasn't Sandy. They're leather shoes and she's a vegetarian."

"What does it mean, being your friend?"

"They're the people I can trust not to hurt me." She gave him a cold look. "I hope you're not planning on trying to chat me up. I'd hate to see you waste all that effort."

James had thought there wasn't a girl he couldn't chat up, until he met Theresa. The fact that he couldn't win her over with a few sweet words like all the others made him like her even more. He worried about that. We just talk, Michael had said to James. He was only beginning to understand what that meant: "How much do you trust Mike?" he asked. Talking to them, he thought. Not chatting them up. Conversing. Exchanging views. Talking!

"That's between me and him," she said, curtly.

"Point taken. Change subject," James said. "What do you like to do when you're not working?"

Theresa thought. "Read. Talk. Think," she said.

James was determined to keep trying. Nothing was going to happen tonight, but he wanted to know where he was for future reference. He still fancied his chances, as usual. "What do you like to think about?"

"Life, Love, and the pursuit of happiness," she said.

"Oh, well that lot should keep you busy." This was not working, he thought. "Your turn to ask the questions," he said.

"Do you want to have sexual intercourse with me?" She looked him straight in the eye. It was working, she thought, assertiveness. She was intimidating him. She could see him wilting in his Y-Fronts. She was enjoying this.

Sweet Jesus, Mary and Joseph, thought James. "You don't mess about, do you?" He was hoping she was joking.

"It wasn't meant as an offer. It was a serious question," she said. "Do you really want to have sex with me?"

He thought he knew what she was getting at. "Alright then," he said, "this isn't a proposition, it's a serious answer. Yes."

"Why?"

"Because you're very attractive."

"So are lots of people." She wasn't buying that. "Do you want to sleep with every attractive woman in the world?"

"Well, if you put it like that, I suppose so, yes."

"Why?"

"Because I'm an incurable sex-maniac," he suggested.

162

"Don't joke! Be serious." She scolded him, trying to stay sounding serious. "Why do you want to sleep with women?"

"Orgasms," he said, thinking that might dent her sensibilities.

She dented his: "Don't need women for those, though, do you?"

She had realised afterwards the meaning of Michael's remarks in the pub the other night. She had played this game with him over that, and it had worked then, too.

"Well no, but . . ."

"Would you take advantage of a girl if she was drunk," Theresa demanded, "or she didn't know what she was doing?"

"I have done," he admitted guiltily.

"Why?"

He finally snapped: "Because I was drunk too, and I didn't know what I was doing then either. Look Treez, I told you before; I'm through with treating girls like that. I'm with Lin now, and I'm very happy with her, and I'd like to be on good terms with you as well, but I'm dammed if I'm going to put up with all this man-hating stuff!"

"Sorry," she said.

He was annoying, this one, she thought; just like her brothers. But she didn't want to hurt him. She wanted to find out more about boys, and she wanted them to understand too. She was only out to graze, not wound.

"Alright," said James. "We'll call a truce, shall we?" He looked at his watch. "I'd better be getting you back." He started the car, and began reversing, very carefully, back to the road. "No girl's ever been late with me," he said, but his gem-of-a-line sounded completely flat.

"Have you had many girls?" Theresa tried to sound more friendly.

163

"Girlfriends, you mean?"

"No, I meant have you had sex with any of them?"

The School Romeo came clean. "Never," he said. "I thought for a minute that one girl I know asked me, but I didn't have the bottle to take her up on it."

"It's nothing to be ashamed of. I think we should be proud of virginity, at our age."

"I know," said James. "But don't tell Mike, OK?"

Michael came back to the table, to find that Lin was already well on her way through the second carafe of wine.

"Oi, you," he said, "save some of that for me."

"There's plenty left," she said. "Did you get them?"

"Yes, I got them."

"Let's see them, then." She held out her hand.

"I don't see why you should. I mean, if you were meant to have them, they'd put them in women's bogs too, wouldn't they?"

"They do, in some places," she said.

"Well I don't think that's right," said Michael. "Not unless we're allowed to have those cotton-wool cigars as well."

"Show us," she demanded.

"Alright," he said, and threw the packet at her. She opened it up, and took one out.

Michael began to get worried: "Sis, there are people who can see us here."

"I'm only taking the wrapper off," she said, and did, in a manner suggesting that this was not the first time she had ever handled one. "I'm not going to blow it up and let it go across the room or anything." Michael was not so sure that she wouldn't. "There you are," she said, throwing it to him, unrolled, "that's what they look like."

"I did know that."

"I bet," she said, "that's the first one you've ever seen in real life, isn't it?"

"No it's not," he said. It was.

"And you know what they're for, I hope?"

Michael thought he was being insulted here. "Yes. For keeping the stumps dry when rain stops play in the test match."

"No they're not," said Lin.

"Well why do they come in threes, then?"

"They're to stop all the little tadpoles from escaping," Lin declared.

"Yes, I know," he said.

"All the little tadpoles that come jumping out," said Lin, "when you play Train In The Tunnel."

"Yes, Lin," said Michael, humouring her.

"And that's where babies come from," she said.

"I know where babies come from, Lin," said Michael. He had been told this by his mother, and on several occasions at school. He found it a bit difficult to come to terms with being told it once again by the baby sister.

"Where do they come from then?"

"Mister Stork puts them under the gooseberry bush . . . nine months after . . ."

"Nine months after you've played Train In The Tunnel, you mean."

"And before you ask," said Michael, "yes, I do know how."

"Everyone knows how." Lin waved the suggestion away. "It's the same as riding a bike."

No it isn't, thought Michael. Or did she know something he didn't? It was possible, he thought, but he didn't think so.

"The important thing isn't how," said Lin, "it's when."

"I know that better than you do," said Michael. "In fact, it was me that told you. Remember?"

"Alright then," said Lin, "remind me, just so's I know you know," she said. "When do you do it?"

"When you're sure," said Michael. "When you're sure you're sure. When you're absolutely sure that you're sure you're sure. When you're so sure that you couldn't possibly be more sure," he said. "Otherwise lay off it."

"That's right," she said. "And when you know that you're sure . . .?"

"You get in there and give it everything you've got," he said.

"Well, goodnight Jimmy," said Theresa, showing him to the door. "Thank you for the lift, and everything."

"Thank you for inviting me into your mansion," said James.

"It's just a house."

"It's twice as big as ours or the Dobsons." James had always wondered what it was like inside the big houses along what was known locally as Millionaires' Row. "Your mother makes nicer coffee than Lin, tell her."

"The dog can make nicer coffee than Lin!"

"I think your Mum might have got the wrong end of the stick in there just now."

"I know," Theresa grinned. "She's just asked me if you were my young man?"

"What did you tell her?"

"I said you were just a friend, but I don't think she believes me."

"Wishful thinking on her part, I'd say. All the mums go for me."

166

"She," said Theresa, "has been trying to get me on The Pill since I was fourteen. I'm a great disappointment to her."

"So what about these rankings of yours, then?"

"What? Oh, well the dog's definitely on the way out, and you're definitely on the way up, now."

"Do you think I'd ever make Number One?"

"Not if you carry on saying things like that, you won't."

"I'm getting the message."

"See you in school," she said.

"Right," he said. "I don't think Mike or Lin need to know where we went tonight, do you?"

Theresa agreed. "Best be diplomatic."

"What? Lie, you mean?"

"No," said Theresa, "just be economical with the truth."

"OK then Bigbruv?" Lin clutched him around the waist as they walked back down the High Street together, on and off the pavement, in and out of the road.

"Yeah," said Michael.

"Do you remember when we used to be friends?"

"No."

"Oh you do," she said. "We used to have play-fights, remember?"

"I wasn't playing," said Michael. "I was trying to kill you."

"You used to read me stories."

"Only to shut you up."

"And you used to take me over the park," she said, "across the main road."

"Used to leave you there too," said Michael, "only you kept finding your way back home."

"What about when you rescued me from that boy in

the playground, what did you say to him? You put my Sis down, you said . . ."

". . . No one beats her up except me," said Michael, finishing for her.

"But then you got really nasty with me. Why was that?"

"You changed."

"How did I change?"

"You know." He was getting embarrassed.

"No I don't," she said.

"You do!"

"I don't. Tell me."

"Before," said Michael. "I could tickle you and I could make you laugh whenever I wanted, and cry whenever I wanted. It was easy; I just had to call you a couple of names, and you'd burst into tears. Or I could do a funny voice, and then you'd get a gigglefit." Lin sniggered. "No, you can't do it anymore," he said. "You've been impossible. I do something, and there's no telling whether it's going to make you laugh, cry, kiss me, kick me, scream your head off, or not talk to me for a week. I preferred you before. Can't you go back or something?"

"I really want you to get off with Treez," Lin said, after a pause.

"So do I," he admitted.

"You just play it like I told you," she said, "and you can't go wrong."

A strong headlight shone on their backs. Michael looked around, and a horn sounded. The car pulled up next to them, but it was only when the driver wound down the window that Michael finally recognised who it was.

"Evening, pedestrians," said James.

Lin cried out when she saw him: "You passed!"

"Of course I passed. I always knew I'd pass. Didn't you?"

"You swine," said Michael. "You lucky, lucky swine."

"Oh, you still want to walk home do you, Mike?"

"No I don't!" Michael ran round to the passenger side, and pulled hard on the handle. The door would not move. "Open the damn door, McGarvey," Michael demanded. James flicked the catch, and in a flash Michael sat next to him. "OK, Western Imperialist Pig," said Michael the fundamentalist terrorist, holding his finger to James's head, "take this plane to Beirut, or we kill all the passengers."

"There are no passengers," said James, glancing towards the back seat.

"Well don't just sit there," said Michael; "get some."

James got out of the car, and pulled the seat forward for Lin to get in.

"Why can't I go in the front?" she moaned.

"Because you are not the pilot or the hijacker," said Michael, his Arab accent beginning to sound a bit Spanish.

"You'll get your chance," said James, "tomorrow night." She climbed in, already looking forward to that prospect.

"Where have you two been then?" James asked, as if he didn't know.

"Argie Pub," Lin sang out from behind.

"On the piss," Michael echoed from in front.

"Good, was it?" James enquired.

"Alright," said Michael, "if you like that sort of thing."

"I do," said Lin.

"I've noticed," said James, "but if you think that this is going to be a taxi service for drunks . . ."

"Then you're absolutely right," Michael declared.

James had a horrible premonition that this might well turn out to be the case.

"Ssssh," Lin called, between giggles. "They're in bed."

Michael opened the front door, and the three of them tried to go in quietly, Lin failing spectacularly in this respect.

"Oops." She nearly knocked over the hall table. "I'll make the coffee, shall I?" She headed off towards the kitchen.

"Quick. Stop her!" Michael was afraid that she would either electrocute herself, or poison them. James hurried off to catch her.

As Michael hung his coat up, he could hear the giggling from the kitchen getting steadily louder. He went to investigate.

"Not now, McGarvey!" Michael found James and Lin all over each other.

"I'm not doing anything." James raised both hands in surrender. Lin appeared to be trying to climb up him by an as yet unexplored route.

"I'm going to get her some of that stuff they put in prison tea," said Michael, pulling her off him.

"That's only for men," said James.

"Well there must be some sort of sex-drive suppressant that works on girls?" Michael asked, holding her down.

"What about brown corduroy flares?" James suggested.

"I've got some of those upstairs," said Michael.

"I bet you have."

"I'm keeping them until they come back into fashion, then I'm going to sell them to you."

"Well you'd never wear them yourself if they were fashionable, would you?"

"Make the coffee, Jimbo." Michael looked at Lin, who was beginning to yawn. "I'm going to take this," he said, "into the living room, to lay its little head over a cushion . . . or possibly the other way around."

James and Michael sat and talked for well over an hour.

"It is bloody late, isn't it?" Michael looked at the clock. "Should we bother going to school tomorrow?"

"Oh, I think so," said James. "But I don't think we should bother going today."

It took Michael a few seconds to work that one out.

James looked at Lin, fast asleep on the sofa. "She's out for the count."

"I like her best when she's like that," said Michael. "And so would you, I bet?"

"Not funny, Mike."

"It happens though, doesn't it?" Michael suggested. "Little girls get drunk at parties, pass out, and get carried up to people's bedrooms."

"Not by me they don't," said James, angrily.

"You've seen it happen though, haven't you?" Michael suggested.

"Yes," James conceded. "Twice."

"And what did you do about it?"

"None of my business."

"What if it was your Sarah?" Michael referred to James's elder sister.

"Then it would be my business," James said, "and I'd probably kill the bastard." James was not exaggerating.

"In that case you know how I feel about her," he said, looking at Lin.

"I think the world of her, Mike, and I'd never hurt her," said James.

"I would," said Michael, still fuelled by the wine.

It went quiet for a while, as they both ran out of things to say.

"Does Sarah know you masturbate?" Michael asked,

looking at the sister creature, whom he would have preferred not to know about things like that.

"Do I masturbate, then?" James said.

"Of course you do, you wanker. Everyone who knows how does."

"No, she doesn't know," said James. "But you do, now."

It went awkwardly quiet for a while again then.

Michael broke the silence: "Do you think I could get off with Treez?"

"Get off with Treez?" James said, in a doubtful tone. "You'd have a job."

"Sleeping Beauty reckons I could."

"What does she know?" James demanded. "How many girls has she got off with?"

"Not as many as me," said Michael, haughtily.

"Well, there you are, then."

"She's going to get pissed out of her mind at the party."

"Who? Lin or Treez?" James asked.

"Who do you think?" Michael said, suggestively.

"Not Treez."

"No," said Michael, "not Treez. She's going to be spending most of her time in the kitchen with me. OK?"

"OK," said James. You reckon, he thought.

Chapter 6

"We can't go on meeting like this," Theresa declared, only realising afterwards what she had just said.

"Why not?" Michael asked.

"Because it's too cold."

It was now November, and the icy wind was blowing wet, mouldy leaves all around their legs.

"What shall we do then?" Michael asked.

"Stay inside," said Theresa, "in the warm."

"What? Sit next to Jimmy and Lin through Break while they both count the hairs on each other's eyelashes, or look for bits of each other they haven't bitten off yet?" Michael was un-enthusiastic.

Michael thought he would never have seen the day that James got a severe case of the Gooey-Eyed Disease. It was an act, he had thought at first, all part of his devious plan, to get her knickers down. But it was beginning to look like it might be Real after all.

"Shut up, they're lovely."

"Individually, perhaps, but together, they're getting to be insufferable."

"Jealous?" Theresa chided him.

"No," said Michael. "I don't fancy either of them."

"Well, where can we go, then?"

"Round my house," he suggested. "It's only a couple of minutes up the hill."

"I'm not disappearing home with you," she said, firmly.

"Why? What's wrong?"

"Eyes will follow us," she told him, "tongues will wag.

Conclusions will be jumped to . . . Hands will wander."
She looked at him disapprovingly.

"I don't know what you're talking about," he said, cheekily.

"You're doing it now."

"Doing what?" Michael looked the other way while he drew the material of Theresa's skirt up and down against her leg.

"Get your hand off," she ordered. "Now."

"That's not my hand," said Michael, brazenly. Theresa grabbed the hand and pulled its fingers back hard, the way it had said in her self defence book. "Aaah! That hurt!" Michael cried.

"You said it wasn't your hand."

Michael pulled away.

It had started with the arm round her, once or twice, and she had allowed that, but then he started putting his hand on the bench just as she was about to sit down, and now it was the leg business. "Why do you do it, Micky?" she asked him.

"Because I like having my fingers dislocated," Michael said, nursing his injuries.

"You should ask before you do things like that."

"Can I stroke your leg, Treez?" Michael asked.

"No."

"Can I put my arm around you, Treez?"

"No."

"Can I kiss your bum, Treez?"

"No!"

"Can I hold your hand, Treez?" He pulled a soppy face.

It was no good. She couldn't keep a straight face when he started. "Alright." He grabbed her hand and began to stroke it briskly, as though it were a hamster. "Indoors on Monday, then?" Theresa suggested.

"If you say so, Treez," he said, still stroking.

She patted his hand when he let go. This one wasn't bad, she thought, for a boy.

"How are you and Micky getting on?" Lin asked Theresa, yet again.

"Fine," said Theresa, as usual. The two girls were sitting in the Common Room, eating their sandwiches. It was surprisingly quiet for a Friday lunchtime in school, and there was hardly anyone around.

"Looking forward to the party tomorrow night?" Lin asked.

Theresa didn't really know whether she was or not: "Yes," she said, politely.

"Do you need a lift?" Lin asked, "because if you do, I can ask Jimmy to collect you."

"Thanks, but I can get the bus."

"What about a lift home then?"

"That would be helpful."

"I'll tell him." Lin finished the last of her sandwiches. "You planning on drinking much?"

"I don't know." Theresa hadn't given it any thought.

"I am," said Lin. "This is going to be my final fling. After that, I'm going to cut down. Jimmy says I've got to. He's sick of seeing me plastered."

"Do we have to bring any drink?"

"Would be helpful," Lin echoed her.

"I'll see if we've got any wine I can have. Does it matter if it's only cheap Spanish plonk? We've got lots of that left over from holidays?"

"Bring it," said Lin, enthusiastically.

Theresa's previous experience of these events, her brothers' parties, was quite different to the way it was done in the Dobson family. "I just thought that since it's a special occasion," she said, "Micky's coming of age, you might be having something special, you know."

"Treez, it doesn't matter if it's red or white, fizzy or still, dry or sweet, so long as it's wet and it makes you fall over, we'll have it."

"It definitely does that." Theresa remembered the summer, and spoke from experience.

"Great." Lin munched on her apple. "There won't be many coming," she said, when her mouth emptied. "Micky hasn't got many friends, so I'm having to invite a few of mine to make up the numbers."

That wasn't the way Michael told it, Theresa thought.

"How long's it going on till?"

Lin nodded and pointed, her mouth now full, indicating that this was an important detail. "We're chucking you all out at midnight. Mum and Dad are coming home from Auntie Margaret's in the morning, and we've got to have the place cleaned up for them by then."

"I'll help you do that," Theresa offered, thinking that Lin might not be in a fit state to rinse many glasses by that time.

"Oh would you? That's lovely of you. Jimmy's promised to help as well, so he can take you home afterwards."

"It's the least I can do. Micky's a special friend, and I'd like to make the whole thing go well for him."

"Oh, good," said Lin, thinking.

"And you've been my friend for as long as I can remember, and I'd like to do something for you as well." Theresa saw her friend almost choke on her fruit.

"I love you, Treez," said Lin, earnestly, her mouth stuffed with apple.

"Alright Lin, alright. No need to go over the top."

"Come here, Michael," June called from the kitchen. "I want to show you all this."

Michael came out to the kitchen, and found June pushing carrier bags into the cupboard-space below the sink unit.

"This is the drink. Beer in that one, and vermouth and stuff for the girls in that one. You're in charge of all this. Make sure You-Know-Who-keeps her hands off it until tomorrow night, won't you?"

"Can I put her in the dustbin if she doesn't?"

"No, you can't! The soft drinks are in the garage, and so are all the crisps and nuts and stuff. Lin knows where the cake is. You're not allowed to see that now, and the same goes for the presents."

"Did you get my rocket-launcher?" Michael asked.

"Wait and see," said June. "Now is there anything you can think of before we go that you'll need?"

"Money," said Michael.

"You'll get that."

"More money," said Michael.

"Get a job," said June. "Your sister has."

"I'm not running around waiting on people for pennies," said Michael, distastefully.

"You wait till you really need money, then your attitude will change." She stood up, and went out into the hall. Michael followed. "You're sure there's nothing else?" she asked.

"No. Thanks ever so much, Mum."

He kissed her.

"Alright darling. I can't hang around any longer, your father's waiting in the car. There's just one thing I wanted to say to you:" Big speech time, she thought. "I know we've said everyone out by midnight, and I'm sure that you and Lin are both responsible enough to stick by that, But . . ."

The next part was proving more difficult . . . "I'm no fool, Michael, and I don't imagine that you think I am. While we're gone, we can't prevent you from doing anything, can we?"

Michael was embarrassed. "It's alright Mum."

"I know, darling, I know. But you're going to be eighteen. Lin's sixteen. And things can happen."

Chance would be a fine thing, Michael thought.

"I just want to ask you," June continued, "to remember that this is our home, and you should respect it; you understand what I'm saying?"

"I promise, Mum."

"Just promise me that if anything should happen; well, you will be careful, darling, won't you?"

"Yes," said Michael.

No, thought Michael, he did not have any contraceptives stashed away anywhere, because he had something better than that to prevent any little accidents. It was called standards, he thought.

"I'm not condoning it or anything, but I'm not going to preach to you, am I?" June grimaced. "Not after how I behaved when I was your age, eh?"

Michael was not aware of the details of his mother's youthful excesses except that they had ended with him, the Miracle Baby, born just six months after the wedding, when she was younger than he was now. That was why he had standards, Michael thought, looking at her, because of everything she had brought him up to understand.

"And you will keep an eye on Lin for me?"

"I will," he promised.

"Watch her for me. I'm not sure that she fully understands what's involved."

"Don't worry, Mum," said Michael, remembering, "she's alright."

"You both are," said June. "Both wonderful, and both mine. At least, I think you're both mine. I don't know, perhaps there was some mistake in the hospital?"

"Piss off, you," said Michael, laughing.

"I will," said June, "and I bet I get more drunk than either of you."

"Come home sober, or I won't let you in."

"I promise." She kissed him and did her coat up. "Goodbye darling, have a lovely time."

When she left, Michael shut the front door, and headed up the stairs to his room. She passed Lin on the landing, on her way down.

"Have they gone?" She asked.

"Yeah."

"What was all that about down there?" She had heard something of Michael's pleadings.

"The Sex Speech," said Michael, brushing past her, trying to look as if he was taking it all in his stride.

"Happy Birthday to Me. Happy Birthday to Me." Michael sang to himself as he walked from the front door to the kitchen, carrying a bundle of cards from the letterbox. "Happy Birthday, Dear Sexy Genius. Happy Birthday to Me." He made some tea, put some bread in the toaster, and began to open his cards: "Happy Birthday Michael, from Uncle Alan and Auntie Jean; ten pounds." He put the card down on the washing-machine, and the money into his pocket. "Happy Birthday Michael, from Nan and Grandad; ten pounds." He repeated the process.

Lin came wandering in, dressed ready for work. "Good morning, Birthday Boy," she said. "Where's my tea?"

"Where's my presents?" Michael demanded.

"Not till I get my tea." Michael poured her a cup.

"And toast, I have," she said, taking his as it popped out of the toaster.

"I should be getting breakfast in bed from you, today," Michael complained. He opened another card: "Happy Birthday Michael, from Margaret and Steve, fifteen pounds. Nice one Steve, mate."

"I've got to go out to work to get that!"

"He ha," said Michael. "Happy Birthday Michael, from Nanny Joan, five pounds. Miserable old cow." Lin went out of the kitchen. "Aaaah." Michael read a card: "Hay-py Birthday Mi-kel, love from Jamie."

"What? Steve and Margaret's little boy?" Lin asked, coming back.

"Yeah," he said. "Happy Birthday Michael, from Susan and Bob, ten pounds."

"Here you are, Micky." Lin handed him a card.

Michael ripped the envelope apart: "Happy Birthday Micky, Luv Lin," he read. "I bet little Jamie'll be able to spell better than you by next year."

"There's kisses on it as well."

"Sod the kisses," said Michael, holding it up and shaking it, "where's the money?"

"In here, I think." Lin handed him the big card.

"This is the one," he said, opening it very carefully. "Happy Birthday Michael, Lots of Love from Mum and Dad . . ."

"How much is it?" Lin asked.

Michael held up the cheque.

"Let me see!" Lin cried

"You get off!" Michael held the cheque too high for her to reach.

"What you going to buy?" she asked.

"Don't know yet," he said, stuffing his fortune into his pocket.

She headed through the doorway. "Come on, your prezzies are in here."

"This is from me." She handed him a small package. "It's not a lot."

He turned it over in his hand. "No, it isn't, is it?"

"You know what it is, don't you?"

"Yeah." He unwrapped the music tape he had asked for her. "Thanks, Sis." He gave her a kiss. He could almost hear the purring when he did.

She looked at the clock. "I'm going to be late, hurry up and open Mum and Dad's."

"It's bloody heavy." Michael picked it up. He pulled the paper off it: "It's Jane's!" he exclaimed.

"Jane's what?" Lin wondered who on earth Jane was, and why she had written such an enormous book.

"*Jane's Weapons Systems.*" Michael held the book up. "Everything you ever wanted to know about blowing people to bits," he said, leafing through it.

"Oh," said Lin, "that's nice."

"Where's the RPG-7?" Michael muttered, looking for it.

"I'll see you later, Micky, OK?" Lin was not very impressed by his taste in reading.

"Alright. I might pay you a visit later on. Do I get a free cream cake?"

"You can afford to pay for it, I reckon, and give me a tip."

Michael strode down the High Street, clutching the items he had bought so far. Still plenty of money left, he thought. Across the road, he saw the place he wanted to go next, and set a course for the entrance.

"How about some service around here, then?" Michael said loudly, into the young assistant's ear.

"Good morning, Sir," said James. "Can I help you?"

"That's more like it. Took you long enough to learn how to address me properly, but I'll let you off."

"That's how we're supposed to address customers. You are a customer, aren't you?"

No, Michael thought, I've only come in here to waste your time. "Yes, I'm a customer, a very rich customer."

"Well I'm a poor starving dogsbody on a partial commission, and I've got a car with a dodgy fuel pump at the moment, so your custom is very welcome. Happy Birthday, by the way."

"Trainers," said Michael. "What have you got?"

"Depends how much you're planning on spending."

"Money is no object, Jimbo."

"Then step this way, Sir. Allow me to show you our range."

James opened another box. "And there's these ones. They've got the special pimple-sole."

"What, like your face, you mean?"

"You want it on your foot," James asked, "or somewhere else?" James indicated where he wanted to fit the shoe, somewhere you didn't normally find them.

"Where's the Manager?" Michael demanded. "I'm going to report you."

"Just decide what you want, eh Mike?" James was trying to keep all the boxes Michael had asked to see out of the way of the other customers.

"Well, I quite like these ones." James reached for the

box. "But I think I like these ones too," Michael said. "And these ones are quite nice."

"You're pissing me about, aren't you?"

"Yes," said Michael.

"I've probably missed three definite sales because of you," said James, who was not finding this funny.

"I know," said Michael, who was.

James put the lids back on all the boxes. "If it wasn't your Birthday, you'd be head flushed down the bog in school on Monday." James angrily collected up the boxes, and went to take them back to the storeroom.

"Alright, McGarvey," Michael called behind him, sniggering, "I'll have the ones with the zits on the soles."

"Oi, how about some service around here, then?" Michael demanded from his place.

"Hi Micky." Lin came to his table. "What do you want?"

"Call me Sir," Michael demanded.

"Piss off," said Lin. "Coffee and cream cake, is it?"

"Yeah," he said, "so long as you never made the coffee."

"It comes from a machine."

"So does Anti-Freeze, which is what you put in it, I think."

Lin disappeared for about a minute, and came back with Michael's order.

"What have you bought?" she asked.

"Some music, a new personal stereo, some bits for school, and I've just been mugged by McGarvey for these." He held up his new trainers.

"How much were they?"

"Too much. I've just seen them cheaper somewhere else."

"He gets commission."

"I know," Michael said. "He can bleeding well buy me a drink out of it."

"You're going to get him something for his birthday. I'll make sure of that."

"I'll get him some face-cream, shall I?" Michael said, tucking into his cake.

"You don't get spots, and you don't get fat," said Lin, enviously. "Why?"

"Exercise, fresh fruit and clean living," said Michael. "If you can avoid all of these, you can't go wrong."

While Lin served some other customers, Michael drank his coffee and ate his cake. When he finished, he went to the till, and waited to pay his bill.

"There's your change," said Lin, expectantly.

"Thanks." Michael stuffed it all into his pocket.

"What about the tip then?"

"Oh yes," said Michael; "when you put the coffee down, try not to spill it into the saucer."

Michael was safely back indoors when the snow came, but Lin caught it on the walk back from the bus stop.

"That dandruff of yours is getting worse, you know," he said, greeting her.

"It's terrible out there." She shook her hair like a poodle. "The traffic's sliding all over the place."

"You'll be doing that later on, when you've had a few."

"I'm soaked, so I've got to change," she said. "I'll go and get ready now. You start moving the stuff out of here into the garage."

"What? In this?" Michael protested.

"Just do it," she said, running up the stairs to the bathroom.

"Thanks a bunch!" He grabbed his coat.

Michael came in looking wetter than Lin had. He hauled the last of the bottles into the kitchen, and staggered into the hall.

Lin came bounding down the stairs: "Well; what do you think?" She was wearing one of her sparkly tops with no straps. "Do you think I'm showing too much?"

"Yeah," he said. "Pull it up over your face."

"It's freezing down here."

"That's because I've had the door open, coming in and out."

"Better not turn the radiators on," she said. "It's going to heat up a lot later on. Give me your coat."

Michael took his coat off and handed it to her. It nearly came down to her ankles.

"I'm having a drink." She pushed past him. Michael chuckled, and waited for the discovery.

"It's locked!" she shouted. He sat on the stairs laughing.

"Micky, there's a padlock on the cupboard with the drink in."

"Is there Lin?" he said, incredulous.

"Yes there is," she said, distressed. "Come and look."

He followed her into the kitchen.

"Look!" She knelt down next to it. "It wasn't there this morning. Was it?"

"You must have missed it. Dad put it there; he seems to think we've got an alkie living in this house."

"He left the key, though?" Lin asked, anxiously.

"In the jar." Michael pointed to the highest shelf.

Lin clambered up onto the worktop, and reached for the jar: "It's not in here," she said, tipping the empty jar upside-down.

"Oh," said Michael. "I wonder where he's put it then?"

185

Michael stood back and watched, as Lin searched her way through all the mugs, jars and ornaments in and on top of every cupboard around the kitchen, clambering over all the worktops in bare feet and a dripping anorak four sizes too big for her.

"What are we going to do if there's no drink?" she whined.

"There's all the coke and stuff," Michael pointed to all the bottles of soft drink he had just brought in.

"That's no good," she said, jumping down. She fiddled with the padlock, pulled it, bashed it, and attacked it with a knife. But it was no use; it was a very strong padlock. Michael knew this, because he had bought it that morning. It was meant for his bike, after tonight.

"What are we going to do?" she cried.

"Don't know," said Michael. "Can't go out to the off-licence in this weather, and besides, I've put all my money in the building society."

"I know." Lin cried, "the cabinet."

She ran into the living room. She looked for the key to the drinks' cabinet, but it wasn't where her father usually hid it. It was in Michael's pocket. She began to try to force the lock on the very valuable antique cabinet. Dressed in Michael's coat, she really did look like a tramp in search of a drop.

Michael appeared in the doorway, and from behind his back produced a beer can. He pulled the ring, and took a sip.

"Beast!" she shouted, as he dangled the padlock key in front of her. He had made his point.

"One glass you can have now," he said, "and then you can come and do my hair for me."

"See. It's ever so much shinier if you put conditioner on it." Lin stopped brushing his hair for a moment and drank the last of her wine.

"Bet that was hard," he said; "making one drink last all that time?"

"Ah, shut up." She dug the brush deep into his skull.

"You should go easy on that stuff, you know."

"After tonight," she said. "Jimmy says I've got to or I'll turn into a real alkie."

"Oh, it's Jimmy says now, is it?"

"I think he really loves me," she said, dreamily. Michael indicated what he thought of this by sticking his fingers down his throat.

"You won't be thinking that when you know what it's like," she said, "and you might even find out tonight, if you don't bugger it up with Treez."

"I am not going to bugger it up."

"What have you got to do then?"

"Only spend a little while dancing," said Michael, going through it one more time. "Keep her in the kitchen most of the time, talking."

"Right," said Lin. "What else?"

"Keep filling her glass, but make sure mine lasts."

"And what are you going to talk about?"

"Her," said Michael, "and how much I like her."

"And what do you do when you're talking?"

"Put my hand on her shoulder." He acted this out with her.

"What do you do if she pushes your hand off her shoulder?" she said, doing that.

"Leave it for a while, then put it back." He demonstrated.

"You got it," said Lin, "and when do you make your move?"

"When she stops pushing my hand off," he said.

187

"And you know what to do then?"

"Yes Lin."

"There." She finished with his hair and took two steps back. "You know; you're nearly as sexy as me."

Michael looked at himself in the mirror. "Two of a kind," he said, standing next to her. "Almost like we were related?"

"OK Bigbruv, let's get out there and knock 'em all dead."

"Where are they?" Lin sat on the table, surrounded by nibbles and paper plates.

"It's the snow." Michael leant against the wall. "It said on the radio that most of the buses are off the roads, and those that are running are jackknifed across them."

"I phoned the girls," said Lin. "They said they were on their way."

"What about Jim?"

"He wasn't in," she said, dejected.

The doorbell rang. They both rushed out to answer it.

"Hi fans." Roland was wrapped up like a guy on bonfire night. He took off his helmet, waterproofs, scarf, donkey jacket, other scarf, gloves, and his other scarf. Lin carried it all upstairs.

"You came on that bike in this weather?" Michael was amazed.

"Yeah, it was great, it was. Dodging between all the crashed cars, up the pavement and down the middle of the road."

"You'll kill yourself, you will."

"Got here, didn't I?" Roland said, casually. "Where's the food?"

Roland sat contentedly between plates of food on the table.

"Don't you want a drink, Sonny?" Lin asked.

"Nah." Roland shovelled peanuts into his mouth. Michael buried his head in his hand. Himself, the baby sister and the stomach-on-legs; it wasn't much of a party so far.

The bell went.

"I'll go." Lin jumped up. She was very eager to get to the door first, Michael noticed.

Michael heard screams from the hall, and knew that the Brownie Girls had arrived. Soon, they came pouring into the living room; Paula O'Leary, Clare Hunter, Jill Bryce, Zahira Qasim, and also Sarah McGarvey. They stood together in a huddle.

"Happy Birthday Micky." Jill stepped forward. "Here's your card." She returned to the giggling ranks.

Michael could tell from the way that they were all looking at him that they were up to something. He opened the card and read it. It was signed by them all, and covered in quite unrepeatable messages.

"Thanks a lot," Michael said to them. "I'll try to do a few of these things to you before the night's out, shall I?" he suggested, thinking that might worry one or two of them.

"Lin said you wanted a kiss," said Clare, "and since it's your birthday, I thought, why not?"

"It's not actually my birthday until tomorrow," said Michael, defensively.

"Well, wait till midnight . . ." Clare edged towards

189

him, "and then we'll do all those things on the card, shall we? When you're officially eighteen? Not a boy ... anymore?"

"If you like," Michael was terrified.

"But now, you get the kiss." She hung herself around his neck, and pulled his head down level with hers. She pressed herself hard against his lips, with one hand on his jugular, and the other arm right round the back of his head. He couldn't move. He couldn't breathe. He didn't care.

Michael wasn't sure whether it lasted for one second or twenty, but when it ended, Clare threw his head back against the wall, leaving him with temporary concussion, and scratch-marks behind one ear. The girls all laughed uncontrollably.

"Did you get him?" Lin asked, hanging on the door-frame.

"Yeah," said Clare. "Can I borrow him again sometime, Lin?"

Michael nodded vigorously.

"You keep your hands off him," said Lin. "You might do him a damage."

"I don't mind," Michael volunteered.

"No, Micky," said Lin, "I've got something even better lined up for you next."

Michael licked the lipstick off in anticipation. "Well, let's have it then."

"Right," said Lin. "Grab him!"

Michael was held by four girls, without him struggling very much. What was going to happen, he wondered? Then he saw, and started to struggle for real.

"Look, Micky," said Lin, dragging it in. "You know what this is, don't you?" Michael pulled and kicked, but there were too many of them for him. "It's a dustbin, isn't it?" she said, "and you're going in it, aren't you?"

190

Michael cried out: "Sonny! Help!"

"No fear," said Roland. "That lot flushed me down one of the girls' bogs the other day."

"In we go, Micky," said Lin, and they lifted him up, eventually forcing him down into the container. Michael writhed and squirmed, rocking the bin over onto its side. He wriggled his way out, stood up, and looked around for Lin. He spotted her, and began to bear down on her.

"Oh come on, Micky, it was only a bit of fun," she said, dashing for the door. He chased her out into the hall, and was just about to drag her upstairs, feet first, for a shower down the toilet, when the bell rang. She managed to get away while he was distracted, and opened the door.

"Jimmy! My Hero, you've saved me," she cried, sheltering behind him as he came inside.

"I said I'd buy you a drink, Mike. That big enough for you?" James handed Michael a two litre bottle of beer. Lin pulled the coat off James and ran upstairs to safety with it. "And that's your card." He handed it over.

"Thanks Jimbo," said Michael, opening it, thinking that the sister creature could be got at his own convenience at some stage when she least expected it. There was no hurry.

"How about pouring me some of that, then?" James suggested, eyeing the drink.

Michael led him to the kitchen. "If you'd care to step this way, Sir."

"So, Mike," said James, between mouthfuls of beer; "what does it feel like to be a man?"

"I'll tell you tomorrow." Michael was holding a half-empty can of flat beer, watching the dancing in the centre of the room.

"What's up?" James asked. "Or can I guess?"

"She's not here yet, is she?"

Zahira broke away from the circle, and came over to the boys. "Come and join the dancing, you two."

"Leave it, Zed," said Michael.

"Come on, Jimmy." Zahira tried to pull him to his feet. "Lin won't mind."

"Hoppit," James told her, sending her on her way. "Have you got her phone number?" he asked Michael.

"Ask Lin," he suggested.

"Do you know where she's got to?"

"Where do you think?"

Lin sat up on the worktop, surrounded by bottles. She waved her empty glass around, and read all of the labels, deciding which to try next.

"What's Treez's phone number?" James asked, finding her.

"Don't know," said Lin, "I'll ring her up and ask her, shall I?"

"Don't muck about Lin."

"I know, I know. I'm not drunk yet." She was working on it though, James thought. "In the little book on the hall table," she said.

James found the book and the number, and dialled. "Hello, is Theresa there, please?" he asked in his best voice, remembering to pronounce the name right. "Hi Treez," he said in his normal voice, "it's Jimmy here; you coming to this party or what?" She said something about buses he couldn't quite hear above all the noise in the background. "Wait there," he said, "I'll come and get you."

"Don't worry, Bigbruv," Lin said, clinging to him as they danced together. "She'll be here soon."

"Why didn't she come, though?" Michael asked, anxiously.

"The snow."

"Why didn't she phone?"

"She doesn't know the number. Same as you didn't know hers."

Michael looked around him at the revelry and mayhem. "Who are all these people at my party, Lin?"

Lin searched for faces Michael might not know: "That's Polly's boyfriend she's dancing with . . . Over there's Sue from where I work . . . See that boy over there with Jimmy's sister?"

"What? The one playing hunt-the-peanut inside her clothes?"

"He's her boyfriend," said Lin. "I think."

"He is now," said Michael.

"And everyone else is from school, so you know them."

"Do I?"

Michael felt himself taking more and more of the weight of them both. "If you're sick," he said, "you're cleaning it up yourself."

"Don't worry, Bigbruv, I only puke up over people I don't like. So you're alright."

"Here we are," James parked the car. "I'm on the lemonade for the rest of tonight; I must be just about on the limit as it is."

"You didn't have to come for me." Theresa was worried that he had risked his licence for her sake.

"Was it the snow," James asked, "or some other reason as well?"

"The snow seemed like a good excuse." She knew she couldn't fool him about what was going on.

"It's to do with Mike, isn't it?"

"Yes," she admitted. "Lin's been dropping hints all week."

"You don't have to do anything if you don't want to, you know?"

"I don't know what I want to do."

"You make it sound so important. You're not expected to offer him unrestricted exploration rights."

"I'm not a North Sea oilfield, Jimmy."

"No, you're not. You're a very impressive and attractive girl." She looked at him disapprovingly. "Correction: young woman," he said.

Theresa was dismissive. "Plenty of them around."

"Plenty of us incredibly handsome and extremely virile young men around as well," said James, grandly, making her laugh.

"It's the Welfare State," she suggested, "all that free milk and orange juice."

"And we're worth more than BP, Shell and Texaco put together," said James, so smoothly you could use him for a non-stick frying pan.

"No wonder you get such low marks for your Economics essays," she suggested.

"I don't take them seriously. And you shouldn't be taking this so seriously. Go on; get in there and give it to him." He leant across and made the lightest possible contact on her cheek. "Lucky sod, he is," said James, breaking away. He pulled the keys out of the ignition, and got out of the car.

"Treez!" Lin screamed when she opened the door.

"It was the snow, Lin; the buses . . ."

"Never mind, never mind, never mind!" said Lin. "Get in here. Get your coat off. Get a drink!"

"I've brought this." Theresa handed Lin a very large bottle of wine. Lin cuddled it like a teddy bear.

"Where's Mike?" James asked Lin, before she ran off to the kitchen with the wine.

"Hiding in his bedroom." Lin pointed upstairs. "Come on, Treez," she said, waving, "come and get a drink."

"Evening Mike." James invaded Michael's refuge. Michael was lying on his bed, reading his new book. "You'll never get off with that, you know?"

"You could, I bet," said Michael, closing the book. "The crack of dawn's not safe when you're around."

"Dawn? Who's Dawn? Have I met her?"

"There's a lad down there," said Michael, getting up, "With his hand down your Sarah's jump-suit."

"Wouldn't be the first time," said James, cynically.

"She's only just fourteen, isn't she?" Michael asked, concerned.

"Us McGarveys don't hang about." James let Michael through the door first.

"When Lin was that age, I was always pulling them off of her in school. Or vice-versa. But then you'll remember that, won't you?"

"I'll go and say hello to them," said James, "make sure he's not planning on crossing the central reservation."

"You brought her?" Michael asked, coming down the stairs.

"Yeah," James said.

Michael and James came into the kitchen as Lin was pouring some of Theresa's wine into a glass, and all around it.

"Ooops," said Lin, tipping the bottle back up.

"I'll get a cloth." Theresa went across to the sink.

Lin pushed the spilt wine over the smooth surface into her cupped hand. Having collected up most of it, she couldn't think of anything to do with it except raise it to her lips.

"You'll be sucking on the dishcloth before you're finished," Michael berated her, entering.

"Hello Micky," Theresa was busily wiping up the mess. "Sorry I couldn't get here earlier."

"So you should be." Michael tried to sound nonchalant. "Sonny's scoffed all the cake, and you've missed the cabaret, toasts and speeches."

James took a firm hold of Lin. "Hey, You," he said, "how's about a dance, while you can still stand, semi-unaided?"

"I am not drunk," she said, jabbing him in the chest with her finger, "I am just light-headed, that's all."

"Yeah," said Michael; "later on we're going to tie a basket underneath you and go ballooning."

"We'll see you later, Mike." James steered Lin through the door.

Suddenly they were alone.

Theresa put the cloth back on the draining board, and wondered where she should go. "What did you get for your birthday?" she asked, awkwardly.

Michael stood by the fridge, half-hiding behind it. "Not much," he said; "except money, which is what I always ask for."

"Same here." She lifted herself up to sit in Lin's place, among the bottles, now mostly empty. "I can never explain to people what I want."

"Christmas is good," said Michael. "I get six million pairs of socks."

"I get loads of those soap and talc sets," she said. "I never use them all."

"Best to stay dirty," said Michael, nodding. "The smell scares the germs away."

"I forgot to get you a card. Sorry." Her nerves were beginning to show as she struggled to find things to say.

"S'alright," said Michael. "Give me the money, I can go and get one from you tomorrow morning."

"It's silly isn't it? The way everything's supposed to change, just because you've reached a certain day, an exact number of years after the day you were born?"

"It's all a conspiracy by the manufacturers of little candles and pink and blue icing," Michael suggested.

"Sex-stereotyping again," said Theresa, almost shivering with nerves. "When I was sixteen, I remember waking up and wondering whether I was supposed to feel any different?"

"I'd have come round and checked that for you," Michael joked, then wished he hadn't. Everything Lin had told him had gone completely out of the window.

"Do you ..." She wanted to say it, but the words wouldn't come out. He was leaning on the fridge, with almost the whole kitchen floor between him and her. She tried again. "Do you want to sit down," she asked, pushing some bottles back from the edge, "over here?"

The look they exchanged as he crossed the floor contained more than a whole evening's conversation, but they were both transmitting, not receiving, and so neither of them got the message.

197

Michael placed himself in the space cleared by Theresa. He felt himself sitting on a wet patch left over from Lin's spilt wine. He tried to ignore it.

Theresa grasped his hand. "Micky, we're friends, aren't we?"

"Yeah." He was looking hard at her.

"That means we don't ever hurt each other," she proposed.

"I'll tell my fingers that was just your way of being friendly, shall I?" He looked down at her holding his hand, and wondered which joints she might pull out this time.

"I'm sorry about that, but what you did hurt me too."

"Show us the bruise, then."

"You're doing it again," she said. "Don't treat me like I was some object provided for your amusement, because I'm not."

"I didn't think you'd mind, that much," said Michael, apologetically.

"Well try to think a bit more in future," she said. "That's your trouble; you don't think. You should think a bit more about yourself, and your work, as well as how you treat other people."

"Yeah." Michael was by now doing an excellent impression of a blancmange.

"You're special, Micky. You've got talent. Don't waste it." She paused for a second. "I wouldn't want to see you waste it," she said, getting as close to saying it as she could.

"Treez, I really want to put my arm around you," he said, awkwardly.

"It's not what you do," she said, lifting his arm around her, "it's the attitude behind what you do that counts."

"I know." Michael's mind was racing and hallucinating.

198

I'm a raspberry jelly, he thought, and you're a pink blanc-mange. I'm a sherry trifle, and you're a chocolate sponge. Michael was sure he was going mad. She was driving him mad. Her. The Girl.

"Don't use people," she said; "and don't let them use you; not for anything. That's what the Lie's all about. You told me that."

This was it, she had decided. It was now or never. This one would do, she thought. He'll do for me.

"You know, I reckon it would have been a whole lot simpler if you'd been a boy," said Michael, "then we could have been mates, without any of these complications."

"Why is it me that's got to be the boy?" Theresa asked. "Why couldn't you have been a girl?"

"What? In a world full of randy males like this is? No fear."

"So you do understand. That's good." He'll do, thought Theresa. He's the one.

"Actually . . ." Michael looked at her closer, "I've had second thoughts. I think I quite like this arrangement." Michael was a bit worried that his naughty little friend didn't seem to be interested at the moment. That can't be right, he thought. But he certainly wasn't going to hang about on that account.

"What arrangement?"

"Us having buttons that do up the opposite way to each other."

"So do I." She placed her hand on his leg, and ran the material of his trousers up and down against it. Hello little friend, thought Michael. Glad you could join us. He leant forward, and tried to get her head in a Clare Hunter Clench. "No," she stopped him. "Not yet."

He was confused. 'Not yet' was an implicit yes. What was she waiting for? Choirs of Angels? Fireworks through the kitchen window? It was something much more practical than that.

"Let's get properly drunk, first." She picked through the bottles, separating the empties from the partially-empties. He joined her in this task. There wasn't a lot left. But there was enough for them. "You take the beer, I'll have the wine." She poured some of her own Spanish plonk into a half-pint mug. "Cheers," she said, raising her glass. This ought to do the trick, she thought.

Bloody hell, thought Michael, watching her. He reached for James's beer. Sorry little friend, he thought, knowing what this was going to do for him. Better luck next time. Next time? Forget next time, thought Michael. This time. This Time. The First Time. Michael started drinking.

"I want another drink." Lin was trying to get out of James's embrace.

"You've had plenty already," he said, "and besides you can't go in there, remember?"

"Why not? He's my brother, she's my friend. We wouldn't mind if it was us."

"Here Lin . . ." James's sister was next to them on the sofa, "have some of mine." She held out her glass.

"Oh thanks Sarah." Lin grabbed a mouthful.

Sarah looked down on her brother from her place on a boy's lap: "This is a first for us Jimmy. Mixed Doubles."

"Vodka and Bacardi," Lin proposed. "That's a good mixed double."

Holding Lin down, James winked at Sarah. The boy moved his hand. James reached out and wrenched it off her. "I've told you, haven't I?" he said, leaving the boy in no doubt. The boy put his hand back on her waist. Sarah McGarvey gave her brother an angry scowl.

The distraction allowed Lin to escape. "I'm going to go and have a look at them." She wriggled away from him.

The kitchen door opened a tiny fraction, and Lin peeked in.

"But surely," said Michael, "if Einstein was right, and it is impossible to exceed the speed of light, then interplanetary space travel can't be a practical proposition . . ."

"But the theory of relativity doesn't allow for what we now know about quantum mechanics," said Theresa. "If particles can appear out of nowhere, and disappear back into nowhere; then it must be possible for spacecraft to do the same, entering some other dimension to arrive instantaneously at a completely different point in the universe . . ."

Lin shut the door, totally bewildered; was that what 'A' Level students did instead of necking each other, she wondered? She headed back to the sofa.

On the other side of the door, Michael and Theresa spat mouthfuls of drink all over each other in their efforts not to laugh out loud.

"OK," Theresa declared, putting down her glass. "I think I've had enough. How about you?"

Michael tried unsuccessfully to down the rest of his beer in one go. He choked, indicating that that was enough for him.

They pushed the encroaching bottles back once again, and sat as close to each other as possible.

Michael ran his finger down the side of Theresa's face, onto her neck, and across her shirt collar.

"Wait." She stopped him from going any further. She placed his hand steady on her shoulder. "Not here. Alright?"

"Whatever you say," Michael swore to her, staring intently into her eyes.

"How about you?" she asked.

"Anywhere you like." She shook her head, indicating that she had no intention of following what he was suggesting by his expression.

Theresa leant heavily on Michael's shoulder, and tried to climb up onto the worktop. She slipped, sending bottles toppling, one of them onto the floor where it smashed.

She tried to get up again, this time successfully. She knelt next to him with his hands supporting her. She took her glasses off, and put them safe up on the shelf.

They started to kiss.

There was a knock on the kitchen door.

"It's Lin," Lin shouted from the other side. "Everyone's gone home. Can I come in?"

They said she could.

Lin beamed from ear to ear when she saw them together, despite the fact that she wasn't feeling at all well. Michael had his shirt hanging out, Theresa's was half-undone. They smiled back at Lin. Theresa tried to do up a couple of buttons, but could only manage one. "We've got to clean up," Lin said, noticing the broken glass all over the floor.

Theresa jumped down, and went over to where her friend was standing. They hugged each other, and exchanged mumbled incomprehensibilities together. They were both very drunk.

Theresa eventually broke away. "I've got to go to the loo." She fumbled her way into the hall without her glasses, a tricky enough task for her even when completely sober. The call of nature was urgent.

"Jimmy's taking Sarah home," Lin explained. "He'll be back soon."

"Well . . ." Michael surveyed the mess all around him; "we drank all the drink, so we're drunk." He laughed. "The drunks drunk the drank and got dronked."

"Stop it," Lin waved at him. "We've got to clean all this up." She bent down to the sink cupboard and got out the dustpan and brush. She began to sweep up the glass, hoping it would take her mind off the pounding in her head.

"My Sis," said Michael, looking down at her. "My lovely, lovely Sis who gave me all sorts of handy hints and advice, about how to get off, and you know what? They were all bugger-all useless when it mattered! I still love my Sis, though. She's the best Sis in all the world. She's SuperSis!"

Lin did not respond in any way, she just carried on clearing the floor. She collected most of the glass, and tipped it into the bin. She went out to the living room to collect some glasses, hoping that if she kept busy, it wouldn't happen.

Left by himself for a moment, Michael came back down to earth. When Lin returned, he was already rinsing glasses.

Theresa was very carefully negotiating the stairs when the doorbell rang. "I'll go," she shouted.

"Hi Treez," said James, as she let him in. "Everything alright?"

"Fine." She smiled at him. "Bit dizzy, that's all."

"I'll take you home in a minute," he promised.

"Thanks for bringing me." She swayed on her feet. With her poor eyesight and the effect of the wine, she was recognising him by voice alone.

"All part of the service," he told her, cheerily.

"I'm sorry if I've been rude, to you, sometimes, Jimmy," she said, hanging onto the banister rail.

"I was the one that was rude," said James. "I owe you a lot. You helped me to see how badly I treated girls, sorry, young women."

"You're alright, Jimmy," she said, woozily, swinging on the stair rail.

"You're not so bad yourself, Treez," he said. "Here."

He gave her a gentle little kiss.

Theresa let go of the banisters, took a step, and stumbled. James held his arm out, and saved her from falling. His hand had a full grip of her by the breast, a complete accident.

She looked up at him, unable to focus, and seemingly unable to move. After what seemed like an age, he began to move his hand slightly, but not to take it away. She stared up at him cross-eyed and helpless. She had drunk herself into what she had told him so many times he shouldn't think of her as. She was putty in his hands.

Theresa was a long way from being in full control of herself, but James could not have offered that excuse. If it had been something he had been planning, he could have tried it later on in the car. As things were, he really didn't know why he did it. He just did, much as he'd done several times before at parties, with girls who were drunk. Even though he felt bad about it afterwards.

"Jimmy!" Lin's scream nearly brought the house down around her.

James looked round and let go of Theresa, who reeled back onto the banisters. She had seen everything happening to her, but it was like she was six foot up in the air and watching it happen to someone else. She couldn't believe it, but she had just let him do it.

"You bastard!" Lin shouted. "You filthy bastard!"

Michael came out of the kitchen to see what the noise was about. Lin began to cry.

"Lin, it's alright." Theresa staggered towards the sound of her sobbing. "It's not what you're thinking." She was back on the ground now, just about. She didn't care about him, though. She wanted to see her friend.

Lin didn't know whether to hit Theresa or hug her, so she did both. She collapsed into her arms. While Theresa stoked her head, Lin sobbed frantically into her friend's shirt. Then it happened.

James ran to the kitchen. "I'll get a cloth."

Michael took Lin from Theresa, and led her up the stairs to the bathroom.

James came back with the cloth, and held it out nervously for Theresa. She snatched it, and attempted to wipe the mess off her shirt. It left a stain, and it felt like there was quite a bit inside as well, but she couldn't afford to worry about that now. "Take me home," she said.

Michael came down the stairs as they were on their way out of the door. "Treez," he called, but she didn't answer, hurrying out to the dim shape of the car; slipping over in the snow, and somehow making it into the passenger seat. "Jimmy, what's happened?" Michael pleaded, completely in the dark.

"Tomorrow." James was finding it hard to look him in the eye. "I'll get her home," he said. "You look after Lin. Say sorry to her for me." He shut the door behind him, and went to the car.

205

Michael sat on the stairs and listened to them drive off, above the sound of his sister's crying from the bathroom.

Michael decided the rest of the mess downstairs would have to wait until morning. He undressed and got into bed. He wouldn't be able to sleep, he thought.

He heard a noise. He had managed to drift off into unconsciousness for a while, but now he was fully awake again. The noise repeated itself, a sort of dull thump. There was footsteps; he would have known whose they were, even if there hadn't been anyone else home. Slowly, he saw the door swing partly open.

"Can I come in, Micky?" she whispered.

"Yeah."

The door opened all the way, and Lin came in, cloaked in a duvet, dragging her mattress behind her.

"You don't mind, do you?" She parked it all at the foot of his bed.

"No. S'alright."

"I don't like it, with Mum and Dad away," she explained.

"I know."

"Night, Micky," she said, curling up.

"G'night, Sis."

They went to sleep.

Chapter 7

Michael got up early on the Morning After, something he had never done before, except under duress. Wandering downstairs, half-awake, he stepped right on the wet patch where Lin had been sick, just after she had covered Theresa. He took his socks off and threw them into the washing basket. Washing, he thought. That was another thing that would have to be done. Quickly.

He put the kettle on, and rushed back upstairs to Lin's bedroom. Where had she put her dirty gear? He found it, eventually; the jeans were OK, but the top was not a pretty sight.

He came downstairs in clean socks, stepping carefully this time, and made himself some tea. He bent down and examined the controls of the washing-machine for the first time in his life. There appeared to be about ninety three different possible programmes, but getting puke off one sock and a purple lurex top didn't seem to be one of them. Michael threw them into the sink and ran them under the hot tap, getting the worst off. That will have to do, he decided, wringing both items dry. He chucked them back into the washing basket. That was close, he thought; for a moment there it had seemed that he might actually have to do some housework.

He heard a noise, the sound of a car pulling up outside, and began to panic. Surely they weren't back this early? He ran into the living room, through a dimly-lit scene of glasses and plates, tables, chairs and cushions scattered at random all over the room. He peered through the gap in the curtains; it wasn't them. It was James.

"Is there anything else that needs seeing to?" James sat with Michael in the now perfectly restored living room.

"Can't think of anything," said Michael. "Thanks for coming round."

"S'alright," James said. "How's Lin?"

"Out like a light. On the floor in my room."

"Did she say anything to you last night?"

"Not a lot that I could make any sense of, except that she's going to murder you."

"Something to look forward to," said James.

"Sounded as if she plans to make it quite painful for you."

"Will she calm down, do you think?"

"Oh yeah. After about a week or maybe a month, or two. Perhaps just a day. You can never tell with her."

James came to the difficult bit. "Do you know what happened?"

"I reckon I could have a good guess."

"I don't know what to say, Mike."

"How about sorry," Michael suggested "for being such a bastard to Lin?"

"And Treez, don't forget."

"I'll see Treez," Michael said. "Find out where we stand."

"Don't blame her, Mike. It was all my fault."

"I didn't see her fighting you off. She got in that car with you afterwards; that's all I know."

Michael and James were still speaking to each other, but there was a hell of a lot they weren't speaking about.

James heard a car pull up outside. "Is that them?"

"Yeah," Michael said, looking out.

"Hello darling," said June, as Michael held the door open for her. "Did everything go alright?"

"Great," said Michael, watching his father putting the car back in the garage.

"Hello," James joined them in the hall.

"Hello James darling. Hope my girl didn't get drunk and pass out on you or anything?"

"No," he said. "Everything was fine."

"No problems," said Michael. Then she appeared.

"Out!" Lin shouted from the top of the stairs. Everyone looked up. For a moment, June thought she was being told to get out.

"Get him out of here! Now!"

Michael met her half-way up the stairs. "Come on, Sis, why don't you go back to bed, eh?"

She pushed him away: "Leave me alone!" she shouted. "And get him out of here!"

"I'll go, shall I." James hurried out of the door, looking very apologetically at June. Not knowing what he could say, he left.

For a while, no one said anything. Then Lin started to sob, and June went to sit with her on the stairs. Lin grabbed hold of her mother. Michael stood isolated in the hall.

June looked hard at Michael. "Shall we talk about this?"

"Treez."

Theresa looked up from her books, and saw Lin standing by her desk. "Hello Lin. How are you feeling today?"

"Can I talk to you?"

"Of course you can." Theresa closed her file.

Lin sat down next to Theresa, propping up a book to look as if she was reading it. "I've got your specs here." She handed them over.

"Thanks." Theresa replaced her old spare pair.

"Did you get home alright, Saturday?" Lin asked.

"Yes," Theresa said. "Jimmy offered to show me to the door, but I said no; spent twenty minutes on the doorstep after that; soaked through and freezing from where I'd fallen over in the snow, trying to get the key in the lock."

"Did you cry?"

"No."

"I did," said Lin. "Were you sick?"

"No."

"I was."

"I know, Lin." Theresa looked at her hard.

"Oh, I'm sorry about that, Treez."

"Doesn't matter. You couldn't help it."

"I got the wrong person," Lin explained. "I wish I'd puked up over Jimmy instead."

"It was a bloody good shot, Lin. You got me right down the neck." She tugged her collar forward to indicate where most of it had gone.

"Oh no," said Lin.

Theresa told the story. "I got indoors OK in the end, though, but obviously I'd got to get myself cleaned up. I managed to feel my way to the bathroom and got myself under the shower, in the end." Lin nodded sympathetically throughout, as Theresa continued to explain what had happened: "By this time, though," she went on, "I'd made rather a lot of noise, of course, and so my mother comes looking for me."

"Does she know what happened?"

"No. She sees me taking a shower, blind drunk, at

one o'clock in the morning, and you can guess what she thinks has happened, can't you?"

"Oh no," said Lin.

"She seemed quite pleased, I think." Theresa took off her mother's manner: "Now you were careful Ter-ai-ser, weren't you, dear, she asked me in the morning."

"Oh no," said Lin.

"But the best bit," Theresa continued, "is that she thinks it was Jimmy, and she wants to invite him round for dinner!"

"Oh no," said Lin, again.

"Stop saying oh no, Lin. It won't make it all un-happen."

"Micky wants to talk to you."

"How is he?"

"He's not saying much."

"And how about Jimmy," Theresa asked, "have you seen him?"

"No," said Lin, curtly, "don't want to, either."

"Is there anything you want me to tell him, if I see him?"

"Yes. Sod off, you bastard," Lin suggested.

"I'll say you don't want to see him for the time being; that sound alright?"

"Suppose so." Lin agreed grudgingly.

"Tell Micky, that I still want to see him . . . but that if he doesn't want to see me, I won't come looking for him."

Theresa had decided that it was a choice between sorting things out with Michael, or going back to her books. If what she was missing was like this she didn't think it was going to be much of a sacrifice to go without it for a bit longer. It had all been quite a shock; but now she was about to get another one of those.

"Treez, what's Feminism?"

Theresa could not recall Lin asking any sort of question

211

like that before, unless it was for some kind of homework. "It's to do with why boys are such rotten no-good pigs, isn't it?" Lin said, "and it says how girls should look after themselves, doesn't it?" she continued.

"Well, sort of . . ." Theresa said. "What is it that you want to know?"

"Feminism," Lin repeated. "I want you to tell me all about it."

There were experienced, dedicated and talented teachers in this school, Theresa thought, who had been unable to get Lin to grasp what a fraction was, or when to use a comma, and now she wanted to tackle Feminism?

"OK," said Theresa. "It starts with the bible, and the story of Adam and Eve . . ."

"I saw Treez this morning. She says she wants to see you."

"Tell her thanks ever so much," said Michael, "but there's no point." Michael was reading one of his football magazines, not looking up at her.

"She still wants to see you," Lin repeated.

"No point," Michael repeated.

"You were soft for her. What's happened?" As was often the case with Michael, Lin was confused.

"So? You were soft for Jimmy, and look what happens when he comes round to say sorry; you chase him off the doorstep!"

"I'm being assertive. Women have to learn assertiveness to combat the sexism of this male-dominated society," said Lin.

"Do you know what any of that means?"

"Yes. It means if he comes round here, I shout at him, and don't let him past the door. And if he ever tries to touch me again, I kick him, in the source of his maleness. I've become a feminist, I have," Lin declared.

"I'll put a sign up on the gate, shall I?" Michael proposed. "Beware Of The Feminist?"

"So why don't you want to see Treez?"

"I do want to see her," Michael at last put down his magazine, "as a friend; a girl-friend, but not a 'Girlfriend'."

"So you don't want a girlfriend?"

"Yes," Michael insisted, "a proper girlfriend. I've never had a proper girlfriend, and Treez isn't a proper girlfriend."

"Why isn't she?" Lin did not understand. "You and her got off together in the kitchen at the party, didn't you?"

Michael shook his head. "We didn't get off together."

"I thought you did!" Lin was now very confused.

"No," he said. "We just sort of . . . you know."

"No. I don't know. What happened?"

"We," said Michael, "well; you know." Lin did not know what on earth he meant. "We just sort of . . . felt about a bit."

"Felt about a bit?"

"Yes." Michael made hand gestures; "you know."

"But that's what you do."

"No it's not," Michael insisted.

"It's what I do," said Lin. "I mean, did do; before I became a feminist."

He told her the story: "It was an enormous joke. We started off all serious; but we were too pissed."

"So?" Lin protested, still not understanding. "Most people are pissed when they get off the first time. I was."

"It wasn't real," Michael insisted. "It wasn't love, and it wasn't even sex, really."

"Well what was it then?" Lin thought that didn't leave much else.

213

"It was a drunken grope, Sis," Michael revealed; "a fumble in the dark. We both didn't know what we were doing until we realised that we were doing it." Michael gave her a meaningful look.

Lin gasped: "Did you and her . . .?"

"Train In The Tunnel?" Michael suggested. Lin nodded. Michael shook his head. "No," he said, "we're not that daft."

"Well from now on," said Lin, "I renounce alcohol, completely."

"I don't," said Michael. "It's probably going to be very useful over the next few weeks; now that I've decided."

"Decided what?"

"I've decided that I've got to lose my virginity." Michael sounded deadly serious, "as soon as possible."

"So has Jimmy said he's sorry to you?" Michael asked Theresa, sitting on their bench together.

"Thirty four times, so far this week," she said.

"And how about me?" he asked. "You want me to say I'm sorry again?"

"No."

They looked at each other, smiled, and fell into an embrace.

She had come looking for him round his house at lunch the previous day. They had missed afternoon lessons and drunk seven cups of tea between them, sorting everything out. Then they had tried it again. From now on, they decided, tea was the only artificial stimulant they were going to use. You might have to dash off to the loo once in a while because of it, but it was even better when you came back. This was more like it, Michael had thought, on the sofa together, with tea, and biscuits! Nothing like sharing a digestive, Theresa agreed. Out on the playing field bench, they were starting again.

"What about the certificate you owe me, Treez?" said Michael.

"First Kiss?"

"That's the one."

"Needs updating now though, doesn't it?"

"Not much!" Michael declared. "What can we put on it? First Kiss, First Snog, First guided tour?"

"You've got some chance," she sneered at the suggestion.

Yes, Michael thought, he had got some chance, if he played his cards right.

"What else was there?" Theresa asked.

"Can't think of anything else," he said. "We never managed the full examination, did we?"

"No; by that time we were incapable of getting my jeans undone between us," she recalled.

"Good thing?" He looked at her very seriously.

"Yes," she said. "If I'd been sober enough to get them open, I wouldn't have wanted them open, Micky."

"Same here," he said.

They both looked at each other, and each sensed exactly what the other was thinking. They kissed. One of their 'A' level Maths kisses; one at a very difficult angle.

"We have still got the problem of Lover Boy and my Sis, though," he said.

"Is she still refusing to speak to him?"

"It's worse than that," Michael revealed. "She says she's given up boys forever!"

"A woman needs a man like a fish needs a bike?"

"Yes, she says that all the time, now. She's thrown away half her clothes, and all of her sprays and gels and things; says she doesn't dress to please men anymore. What did you have to go and tell her all about bleeding feminism for?"

"Bleeding feminism it is," said Theresa. "Only Women Bleed."

"Yes, she says that all the time as well, now."

"Well it's true, isn't it?"

"Not according to McGarvey, it isn't; he reckons his heart's bleeding for her."

"He told me he went to confession and said umpteen hail-wotsits over me."

"Bet that made you feel better?"

"It made him feel better, that's what counts."

"Do it, feel guilty about it, say sorry to the priest, and then forget about it. Catholics I will never understand."

"He says he's rediscovering his faith, because of me."

"Oh great!" said Michael. "Lin's burnt her bra, and he's bin done got religion! I'll give them another week before they're both back slobbering all over each other."

"We should do more than bet on it," she said "we should help it along."

"We can but try," Michael agreed.

"Do you know where Sonny's got to?"

"No." Michael sounded worried, "I haven't seen him since the party."

"He's not been round?"

"No, and he's not been in school either."

"Phone him up," said Theresa; "this afternoon."

"Hello, is Roland there, please?" Michael asked down the phone.

"Is that his name?" Theresa really didn't know. Michael nodded.

"It's Micky, tell him," said Michael. "No. Micky! With an M!" He shouted into the receiver. "His brother," Michael explained to Theresa, with a hand over the mouthpiece; "ugly, thick, and violent."

There was a pause, while Michael waited for Roland to come to the phone. "Hi Sonny, it's Micky," he finally said. "What's up?"

Michael put the phone away from his ear.

"What is it?"

"He's hung up," said Michael, putting the phone down.

"We're going round there," she said, very decisively.

"Do you know where he lives?"

"No," she said, "do you?"

She had misunderstood him: "No, I meant do you know that he lives on the Manor?"

"What's the Manor?"

Michael was aghast: "Bloody hell! You really do live in a world of your own up there on Millionaires' Row, don't you?"

"It's the council estate, isn't it?" Theresa remembered.

"Yes, it's the council estate and by the time we get there it will be dark; and the only people who wander round on the Manor in the dark are druggies, drunks, perverts, whores, and muggers."

"What about the police?"

"Treez, they've got more sense. They stay where it's safe; cruising up and down the High Street, or round your way."

"We'll go tomorrow, then," she said; "in the morning."

"What about school?" Michael asked.

"What about school," said Theresa.

"I've never been up here before," said Theresa, getting off the bus.

"Welcome to the other side of the tracks," said Michael.

"Do we have far to walk?"

"It's that block there." Michael pointed to a less than attractive tower a few hundred yards in front of them.

"What floor is it?" Theresa asked, reaching the entrance hall.

"The fifteenth," he said, "only you don't use the lifts."

"Why not?"

"Because they're full of gluebags, urine and used contraceptives, usually. Did you read in the local paper about the kid who got raped in a lift on this estate, the other week?"

They took the stairs.

"The council want to sell these flats," said Michael, as they reached the fifteenth floor. "It's funny that no one wants to buy them, isn't it?"

"I never knew." Theresa shook her head at the thought of it all.

They reached the flat. Michael rang the bell.

"Do you think anyone will be in?" Theresa asked.

"I have no idea." Michael was wanting to get inside, or else away from the estate, as quickly as he could.

"Does his mother work?"

"In a betting shop, and his brother asks people for money on the street."

"Do they give him much?"

"They do when he hits them over the head," said Michael. "He's coming."

Roland opened the door, and they saw why he had not been at school.

"Fell off me bike, didn't I," he explained.

"Why didn't you phone or anything, you stupid little sod?" Michael demanded, sitting in the living room of Roland's flat. "I thought you'd emigrated, or been carried off by a hungry tomcat or something?"

"I can't use the phone," said Roland, "I've got a bad ankle."

"You only have to pick it up," said Michael, "not tap dance on top of it!"

"I have to use the phonebox," Roland explained. "Our phone's only for people to call us."

"Well, why did you hang up on me, then?" Michael demanded. Roland wouldn't say.

Theresa came in from the kitchen with three mugs of tea. "There's nothing out there," she said, "just powdered milk and some jars."

"I've got some biscuits," said Roland.

"Well let's have 'em, then," Michael demanded; "about time I got some food off you."

"They're in my room, in the bottom drawer."

"I'll get them." Michael stood up. Roland didn't look very happy about it.

"Why don't you have any food in the house, Sonny?" Theresa asked, while Michael was gone.

"Me mum brings stuff in in the evening," Roland explained. "She doesn't keep anything here, because me brother just nicks it all and sells it downstairs."

"When did you come off your bike?" she asked.

"On the way home from the party," said Roland.

"When does the plaster come off, do you know?"

"I'm back at the hospital next week."

"It's the number one cause of death among people our age, road accidents," said Theresa, "and motorbikes are the most dangerous of all. You should stay off it, or get proper training."

Roland thought that he had better tell what had really happened: "I got this from the crash . . ." He rolled up his sleeve, revealing some bad grazing. "The ankle was from being thrown down the stairs by me brother, for smashing up his bike."

"Do you want any of these, Treez?" Michael's mouth was full of digestive.

Theresa snatched the packet from him, and gave them to Roland. "They're all he's got!" She opened her bag and took out one of her school files.

"What are you doing?" Michael asked.

Theresa didn't answer him; she pulled a sheet of file paper out and started writing on it. "This is my address and phone number." She handed it to Roland. "Come round after school anytime, and I'll do you one of my scrambled omelettes."

"You've landed yourself right in it now," Michael told her. "You're going to be eaten out of house and home, before you know what's happened."

"We've got to be back in school before the end of break," Theresa announced, finishing her tea. "You should try to get back as soon as possible," she said to Roland. "I know it's difficult with the stairs and everything, but the longer you leave it, the more work you'll have to catch up."

"I'm not coming back to school."

Roland looked very forlorn, like he was afraid he was intruding on something between Michael and Theresa. It was the way he had looked at her from the very first day. Theresa noticed it, but Michael was about as sensitive as a pneumatic drill.

"What do you mean, you're not coming back!" Michael demanded. "What do you think you're going to do? Get a job as a garden gnome?"

"I'm signing on tomorrow," he said. "I'll never pass any of my exams, and this way I'll have some money in me pocket at last."

"You are a talented artist," Theresa told him, "and you should be on a course of some kind."

"What course?" Roland murmured.

"Come down to the Westone Library with me one Saturday," Theresa told him. "We'll go through all the prospectuses together. We'll find something; I know we will." She gave him a kiss. "See you." She stroked his cheek, then picked her bag up.

"Bye," said Roland. "Bye, Micky."

"See you," said Michael. "Take care."

"You remember I said I wanted to see the world?" Theresa asked Michael, on the bus going back to school.

"Yeah."

"Forget it," she said. "I don't even know my own country yet. My own town, even."

"The Manor's a bit different from Millionaires' Row, isn't it?"

"It's another world."

Michael thought Miss Clever Clogs needed educating: "You've been going to school with kids from the Manor for over five years, you know."

"Yes, but hardly ever coming into contact with them outside the playground."

"That's because you've always been a top set kid," Michael suggested, "am I right?"

221

"Yes," Theresa admitted, "all the time."

"Same as me," said Michael. "Have you ever been past one of those classes where the kids are climbing all over the furniture, and throwing their books out of the windows?"

"Yes. Why?"

"That's where they put the Manor Kids," Michael explained, "those that bother to come to school in the first place. They put Sonny in there right from the start, soon as they saw what his address was. They put Lin in there too, after she failed a few of their tests. Then she failed her exams. Proves their tests were right about her, I suppose they must think."

"Lin was never the academic type." Theresa thought that Michael wasn't being entirely fair.

"Oh, she was never going to get a whole set of pass grades, like me, or a whole set of top grades, like you; but she always liked stories, and she's red hot when it comes to working out how much it's going to cost her to get smashed on different sorts of booze." Theresa laughed. "She could have passed her English and Maths, if she hadn't been thrown in with that lot; the piranha pack."

"What are we going to do about her and Jimmy?" Theresa asked.

"Well Jimmy seems to be shaping up alright now that he's been Born Again. It's my Sis that's the problem."

"There's another school disco at the end of the week," Theresa said; "what if we could get her to come to that?"

"I'll give it a try," said Michael, "but she's been acting a bit funny, lately."

"No! I'm not coming!"

It was as bad as he had feared. The sister creature had turned into a monster, and none of the tricks he normally used on her to make her laugh were having any effect.

"Oh come on, Sis."

"Don't you call me that," she said. "I am only a sister to my fellow sisters."

"You haven't got any sisters, you stupid daft cow!" he said. "Just me!"

"You cannot hurt me with your sexist language, Micky."

"I don't want to hurt you, Lin." Oh yes I do, he thought. I want to wring your rotten little neck, you pest. "I want you to stop all this rubbish and get back to being your old self," he said.

"You mean that other person?"

"Yes," said Michael, "that other person; the one you've got locked up in that room of yours."

"You are not to enter that room," she told him. "That is a Woman's Room; only other women may enter."

"You let the cat in," said Michael, "and he's not a woman."

"He has been made harmless to the women of the cat world, Micky."

Michael did not think James would agree to such a drastic step to get her back; be good fun to ask him though, he thought. Time for some sort of drastic measures though, he decided. "Alright, you," he said, "I don't know who you are, or where you came from, but I say: Get back from whence you came!" Michael made a cross with his fingers, and grabbed a sheet from the ironing basket, wrapping it around himself. "Give me back my Lin!" he demanded, summoning the powers of the supernatural: "She might have been a flasher, a wino, an idiot, a hair-spray junkie, a nympho, a pervert, and a general all-round pain in the bum; but she was still my Sis!" He sat down next to her.

223

"She was good to me. She put up with all the rotten things I did to her. She always wanted to be my friend, even when I called her all the names under the sun, and she made me get off my bum and sample some life. She took me out, and showed me how to have a good time . . . and yes, alright! I loved her," he said, honestly. "Until she turned into a She-Devil!"

Lin's icy stare began to drip, and then melted away. "Oh Micky," she said, nearly crying. She flung herself on top of him. It took him nearly a minute to escape.

"Jimmy dropped me off at the bottom of the hill," said Theresa, as Michael let her in. "He'll be along later."

"Great," said Michael. "Mum managed to rescue all that stuff Lin threw out, so we're alright there."

"That's the next problem, isn't it? Your mother?"

He confirmed her fears: "This is the moment all mothers dream of, and sons dread."

"Has she been briefed?"

"I've told her that if she so much as mentions the M word or the E word, I'm leaving home. She said she'd pack my bag for me."

Theresa was apprehensive. "It's silly, I know, but I've been coming round here for years, and I don't think I've ever said more than hello or goodbye to her."

"Sounds just like me and my Dad."

"What's she like? Your mother?"

"Nutty as a fruitcake."

"Mum, this is Treez."

224

"Short for Theresa."

Theresa offered a hand, and got a kiss on the cheek.

"Hello darling. I knew it would take someone special to make my boy stop sitting up in his room by himself and I was right."

"Told you, didn't I?" Michael said to Theresa.

"Lin's getting ready, Michael," said June. "She said she'd do your hair if you want."

"I'm going to have to do it myself tonight, I think."

"Why's that?"

"All will be revealed," said Michael, looking at Theresa. "We'll see you later, OK."

Michael and Theresa went upstairs, leaving June alone, wondering.

"Look at this!" Michael protested, showing Theresa the sign on Lin's bedroom door: Woman's Room. "Makes it look like a bog," he said.

"You go and get yourself ready," Theresa told him. "Leave us alone."

"Pardon me for my chromosomes," said Michael, going to his own room.

Theresa knocked on the door. "It's only me," she called.

"Hi Treez." Lin opened the door, dressed up to the nines; Ready To Boogie.

Theresa sat on the bed, watching Lin fix her hair. "It's lovely to see you back to your old self, Lin."

"Oh, it feels so lovely, Treez, dressed like this again. But I still feel different. Here, can you hold that like that while I spray it?"

Theresa held Lin's hair the way she wanted it.

"I read those books you gave me; tried to, anyway. You can have them back now."

"Thanks."

"I think I understand some of it, though," said Lin.

"What's that?"

"Well, the sign stays on the door. Micky doesn't come in here anymore, unless I invite him, and I always get dressed before I come out, now."

"That's good, Lin," said Theresa, understanding.

"And from now on; I dress to please me, not boys," she said.

"That's the idea," Theresa approved.

"And one more thing that's different. I'm off the drink, starting tonight."

"That makes me feel a whole lot safer, Lin."

"Apart from that, it's the same old me." She finished doing her hair. "What do you think?" she asked.

Theresa admired her friend's finished efforts: "It's beautiful, Lin."

"Your hair's nice, too. When did you have it done?"

"This afternoon."

"Does Micky like it?"

"Who cares?"

They both smiled.

"Now," said Theresa, "what I wanted to ask you was, what have you got that will fit me, that looks a bit better than this?"

Lin stood up, and surveyed Theresa from head to toe, plain as ever in her sweatshirt and jeans. "Get 'em off," she said.

Michael sat downstairs with his mother, waiting for the girls.

Lin came in from the hall: "Right, I want a fanfare."

June and Michael stood up, and Lin went to stand next to them. "Come in, Treez," Lin shouted. "One, two, three, now!"

The Dobson family gave a hopelessly out of time fanfare, and Theresa stepped in wearing very tight jeans and one of Lin's wilder tops.

"It's lovely, darling," said June. Theresa smiled; she was even wearing some eye make-up. "Well, Michael," said June, "don't just stand there gawping; compliment the girl."

Michael went up to Theresa and studied her closely. "Do I know you?" he asked.

Lin got up: "We'd best be going now, Mum."

"Alright, darling. Have a lovely time."

"We will," said Michael.

"And you're welcome to bring one or two friends back for coffee afterwards, if you want!" June called after them.

The Brownie Girls greeted each other on the dance floor with their usual whooping and screaming, with particular attention this time to Theresa. Michael went to get a drink, and to see if James had arrived.

"Treez Babe, you sexbomb!" Clare said. "Why haven't we seen you looking like this before?"

"You know why," Jill suggested to Clare. "You've had Micky, same as her."

"What was this?" Theresa wanted to know.

"Don't get the wrong idea, Treez," said Paula; "this was before you and him . . . ah'm, ah'm."

"Did you really do *that* to him?" Zahira wanted to know.

"Do what, Zed?" Theresa asked.

"Well that's what we want to find out," said Clare. "Lin's told us what Micky told her, but boys lie their arses off about things like that, don't they? So we want to hear it from you."

The girls all nodded.

"And if you tell us what you've done," said Lin.

"We can tell you everything that we've done," said Paula.

"This is your initiation into the Brownie Pack, Treez," Lin explained. "We couldn't let you in on our secrets while you were Miss Concrete Knickers of the Sixth Form," she said. "Sorry."

"But now that you're the Kenwood Chef . . ." said Clare.

"It does all sorts of different jobs in the kitchen," Jill explained.

"Sounds as if you've won yourself a whole load of Brownie badges," said Paula.

"And we want all the details," said Zahira.

"But . . ." Theresa was dumbfounded; "we can't talk here!"

"Not here, stupid," said Lin. "In the toilet!"

"Come on," said Theresa, and they all ran to the Ladies in a great giggling gang.

"Alright then, Jimbo?" Michael asked, finding James.

"Evening Mike. Where's Treez got to?"

"I have absolutely no idea," Michael told him.

"She'll be in the bog, then," James told him. "That's where they are when you can't find them."

"They must all be in there, then," Michael supposed; "doing whatever it is they do in there."

228

"Do you know what they do in there?" James asked.

"Same as we do," Michael supposed, "with one or two little variations."

"No," said James, "they don't need to go in there that often for that, or that long. And they don't need to go in a coach party, either."

"Well what are they doing, then?"

"Search me."

"Lin's here," said Michael.

"Yeah," said James.

"So then, Jimbo; do you fancy a dance?"

"Not with you I don't."

"What we going to do, then?"

"Well I don't know about you," said James, "but I'm going to go to the bog, and do what I do in there."

Michael attempted to dance on his own, keeping an eye on the entrance, wondering when Theresa was going to put in an appearance. It was Paula O'Leary who came to the edge of the dance floor, gesturing to Michael that she wanted him to come and speak. He went over to her, and she told him what the Brownie Girls wanted him to do.

"Come on, you," Michael said to James, minding his own business sat in a corner. "You're dancing."

"It's very kind of you to offer, Mike, but you're just not my type."

"No arguments," said Michael. "Come on. I think this might just be your lucky night."

Michael managed to coax James onto the floor, and gave the signal to Paula, still lurking in the shadows. Paula signalled to Jill and Clare, dancing near the stage, and they got up and spoke to the DJ. The music stopped.

The DJ read out the special announcement; a dedication to Jimmy, from someone who said she wanted to try again. The slow song started, and she appeared.

The whole centre of the floor cleared as Lin approached James. They stood looking at each other for a moment, just out of reach. Then she took another step, and the dance began. Michael wanted to stay and watch, but before he knew what was happening, he was being carried off the floor by three girls.

"What are you lot all staring at?" Michael demanded, as the girls all gazed at him, standing by the cloakroom area.

"Micky," said Jill, "we just wanted to tell you that we all think you're really horny."

They all nodded.

They were looking at him in a very peculiar way, Michael thought; like they knew something about him that he didn't. He wondered if it was the obvious thing? He checked. It wasn't; his flies were done up. "Well thanks very much, J.B." he said. "You're P.F.A. yourself."

"Pretty Fairly Amazing?" Jill thought she knew that one.

"That's one version of it, yes," Michael said.

"So . . ." Jill was lurking and smirking; "what we all wanted to ask you was; how about some kissy-kissy?"

Michael found himself being kissed by Jill Bryce, then by Paula O'Leary, then Zahira Qasim. The other girls tried

230

to stop Clare Hunter, saying that she'd already had her go, but Michael made sure she got another go. They told him they were off to the dancefloor, to join James and Lin. For a moment, Michael was set to follow them. Then he remembered.

"What are you doing over there, Treez?" Michael asked.

"Waiting for a bus." Theresa was sitting under the cloakroom rails. She had been watching the whole thing.

"Fancy a snog while you're waiting?"

"Might as well. I suppose," she said, trying to keep a straight face.

"And if Lin thinks," said Michael, "that we're going to finish up snogging in the cloakroom . . ."

"Then she's going to be out of luck, isn't she?"

James tapped Michael on the shoulder: "It's time to go home, children."

"What you talking about?" Michael demanded, looking at his watch. "It's not even ten o'clock yet!"

"Oh, just getting warmed up, were you?" James asked.

"Listen, McGarvey, when we get warmed up, you can run your central heating off us."

"We're being chucked out early," said James. "We've just had a big lecture from Mrs Garrett about alcohol abuse."

"Has she caught someone drinking?" Theresa asked.

"No," said James, "but she's been down the dustbins outside."

"Only took her three years to figure that one out," said Michael.

"We've had some trouble in there as well," James said.

"Anybody hurt?" Theresa asked, worried.

"Not physically," said James, "but Lin's down on the

231

steps looking after Zed; kid's crying her eyes out."

"What happened?" Theresa asked.

"Some lads said a few things they thought were ever so funny," James informed them.

"Did they just happen to pick on the only black girl in the Sixth Form entirely by chance," said Michael, very angrily, "or was it what I think it was?"

"What do you think?" James replied.

"We're having their names on Garrett's desk, with all the details," said Michael, "first thing, Monday morning."

Theresa got up. "I'm going to see Zed."

James sat down next to Michael.

"Well, Mike; I never expected to end up in the cloakroom with you tonight."

"Everything OK between you and Lin?" Michael asked.

"Yeah. Thanks for everything you did to get her back for me."

"S'alright," said Michael. "Thanks for touching up my girlfriend when she was too pissed to do anything about it."

"I'm really sorry about that, Mike."

"I know you are, you great daft Catholic pratt, you."

"Lapsed Catholic pratt, if you don't mind."

"I thought you'd seen a vision of the Virgin Mary, telling you to repent?"

"I did, only she told me I had to give up sex until I was married."

"Don't mention the M word!"

"Sorry," said James. "She said I had to give up sex until, dot, dot, dot; then afterwards, she said, the only contraception I was allowed to use was the Irish Pill."

"What's the Irish Pill?"

"It's six foot across and weighs half a ton; you slide it in front of the bedroom door," said James. ". . . And if I couldn't stand that, she said, then tough, because divorce is out the window as well. No thanks Darlin', I said, and she went off to make someone else's life a misery, instead."

"Probably went to see some starving woman living in a cardboard box in the Philippines," Michael suggested, "to tell her off for having that abortion."

"Actually, I still draw the line at abortion, Mike. Life is Sacred."

"Bloody hypocrite, you are!" said Michael; "picking out the bits that suit you, chucking out the bits that don't. Be honest. Come and sign up with us baby-murdering humanists; we're ever so nice. We've not started any wars, yet."

"No thanks," said James. "I'll stay lapsed."

"OK and I'll stay right, shall I?"

"Just thank God for one thing, Mike."

Michael looked very dubious: "Alright. I'll buy it. What have I got to thank God for, Papist?"

"That your mother never had you 'aborted', as you would say."

"I should never have told you about that, you Jock bastard."

"No, Mike; you're the one that's the bastard."

"Not according to the law."

"According to God's Law," said James.

"Hypocrite," said Michael.

"Bastard," said James.

The boys embraced, then got up and headed off in search of the girls.

"You OK, Zed?" Michael bent his knees to look her in the eyes.

Zahira nodded.

233

"What are we gonna do now?" Jill moaned. "Can't go home yet!"

Lin looked at Michael: "She did say we could, didn't she?"

"Only because she thinks we wouldn't," said Michael.

"Shall we?" Lin asked him.

"Yeah," he said.

"Come on everybody," said Lin, "the Disco's not finished yet."

"Well I don't see why it has to be me that tells her," said Lin, opening the door.

"Because," said Michael, "Jimmy doesn't need permission, and they're your Rat-Pack."

"Brownie Pack!"

"Same difference," said Michael.

"Alright then." Lin made sure she had them all in the hall. "Everybody quiet, and only come in when I say."

"Mum," said Lin.

"Oh, hello darling." June did not get up. "You're home early."

"We got chucked out," said Lin. "You know you said it was alright if we brought some people back?"

"One or two people, yes." June didn't like the tone of her daughter's voice. It was her sorry-Mum-I've-broken-it tone, June thought.

"Oh good," said Lin, "because I've brought one or two, and Micky's brought one or two, and Treez has brought one or two as well."

June looked doubtful. "How many?" That was what she wanted to know.

"Come in everybody," said Lin, and seven came in from the hall.

Lin looked worried. Michael tried not to draw attention to himself.

June stood up and looked them all over; six fine young ladies, and two handsome young men. Shame about the numbers, June thought, but you can't have everything, can you? "Alright then," she said, "who wants tea and who wants coffee?"

No one did.

June looked them all over again, and tried to read their minds. She reckoned she could. "Alright then," she said, "who wants gin and who wants vodka?"

June was a mind reader.

"Michael," she said, "go and get the mixers and the orange juice from the fridge." Michael went to the kitchen. "Lin," said June, "open the drinks cabinet." Lin went to the cabinet and reached for where she knew the key was. "A-ha! Caught you!" June cried, pointing accusatively at her daughter. "You said you didn't know where that was!"

Lin backed away guiltily. "I'm off it now, Mum, honest. Aren't I, Jimmy?"

"She is," James confirmed.

"Alright darling," said June, opening the cabinet. "You did tell me, and I believe you." Michael brought the glasses and mixers in, and June began to pour eight single measures. "Now, you girls; would any of your parents object if they knew about this?" Clare, Jill, Paula, Zahira and Theresa all shook their heads furiously. June looked at them all: "Lying cows, the lot of you." She handed out the liquor, and Michael supplied the accompaniments. "Don't get too excited," said June, "all the drink in this house seems to get watered down. James," she went on, fixing her own glass, "put a record on."

235

"Yea," shouted Jill. "Get Down, Mrs D." June had dug out her old Beatles records, and was demonstrating to James and the girls the correct way to Twist And Shout.

"This," she said, "is what we used to call groovy!"

"Is that the same as funky?" Clare asked, trying to copy her.

"Yes, I suppose so," said June.

"Did you used to go to a lot of parties in the old days, Mrs Dobson?" Zahira asked, dancing by her side.

"Two things, Zed darling," said June. "First, not so much of the old days, if you don't mind . . ."

"Oh," said Zahira. "Sorry Mrs Dobson."

"And stop calling me Mrs; my name's June," said June; "or as they used to call me at school, Flaming June."

"Oh Mum!" Lin was finding her mother's behaviour embarrassing.

"Oh, this is my daughter, by the way, everybody." June hugged Lin. "She's ever so nice, but she doesn't like to see me enjoying myself."

The record faded away. In the quiet, a conversation could be heard: "Well, I think we should ask her," said Paula.

"Don't be stupid," said Lin.

"Oh shut up, you," said James.

"Thank you, Jimmy," said Paula.

"S'alright, Pol," said James.

"What's going on?" June sensed they were talking about her.

"Mrs . . . I mean June," said Paula. "How would you like to join our gang; the Brownie Pack?"

"She can't!" Lin cried.

"Just an honorary member," Paula added. "She doesn't have to prove she's earned any of the badges or anything."

"Badges?" June was intrigued.

"Don't you tell her!" Lin cried, getting very worried now. Anything Lin didn't want her to know that badly was obviously worth knowing, June thought. "Tell me all about it when I get back," she said, rushing out the door. "I shan't be long," she shouted from the stairs. "Put another record on!"

June knocked on Michael's bedroom door. It opened, revealing Michael and Theresa standing next to each other, anxious to show that they weren't up to anything.

"Well," said June, standing back, "what do you think?"

June was wearing a genuine original 1967 black and white mini dress. It still fitted her, just about. Michael was speechless. "Reckon I've still got the legs for it, Treez?" June asked.

Theresa watched as June did a twirl: "It's lovely."

"I'm going to have you put away, I am," Michael told his mother.

"This is just to remind you," said June, "that I wasn't born old; I was just like those girls down there. I had my friends. We had fun. And we made a few mistakes." A very big mistake, in her case, June thought, or so it seemed at the time. This, she realised, was the first time she had worn this dress since she learned that she was carrying Michael. "Don't believe all that stuff about parents always knowing what's best for you," she said to him. "We can help, but in the end, you have to work things out for yourself."

"I love you, Mum," said Michael. "You stupid daft cow, you."

"I love you too, darling," said June. "Well, I'm off

downstairs now, back to the dancing before your father gets home, when it will all have to stop. Are you two alright up here?"

"Yes thanks," said Michael. "We're only talking," he added, hoping she didn't mind them being in his bedroom together.

"*Only* talking?" June doubted.

"Well; you know. We won't be doing anything stupid."

"No," said June, "I know you wouldn't."

June Dobson left Michael and Theresa to carry on reliving her misspent youth.

Talk was all that Michael and Theresa did do over the next couple of hours; just talk together, listen to music, eat digestive biscuits! And . . . well; you know.

Some more titles in Lions Teen Tracks: